The Servant Girl's Secret

A Colonial Girl's Story

Jami Borek

The Servant Girl's Secret

ISBN-13 (print) 978-1-7377670-0-8
ISBN-13 (ebook) 978-1-7377670-1-5

Published by:

chapter 1

Jacob woke up suddenly. One moment he was fast asleep and the next moment his heart was racing.

What had awakened him? He lay totally still, scarcely breathing, listening for noises in the dark. Was someone in his room? No, he realized with relief, the noises were outside, in the street below. He could hear men's voices and the snorting and neighing of horses. What were they doing in the street at this hour, long before dawn?

Jacob got up as quietly and crept to the tiny

window in his attic room. From the direction of the noises, he could tell that there were men by the Armory. It was a small red-brick building with a wall around it and a heavy door. Set apart in a grassy square, the Armory was a secure place where the town's weapons were stored.

There was no moon and it was very dark, but some of the men carried torches. He could see that some of them wore red uniforms and carried swords. There seemed to be a lot of men — ten, maybe even twenty! They were taking things from the Armory and loading them into the wagons.

The Armory was supposed to be guarded by the townspeople of Williamsburg. These men weren't townspeople, though. He didn't know exactly what was going on, but he knew that it was wrong.

He wondered what to do. Should he wake Doctor Galt? Should he yell at these men who'd come in the night to take things away?

Then Jacob heard the drums, rhythmic and loud. Someone else must have seen the men also. They were beating out an alarm to wake the town.

Soon men from the town were running down the street, angry and shouting. From every side, more and more men were joining them, awakened by the drums. By now, the men in uniforms had stopped loading things and the wagons were on their way. The British marines — for that's who they were, Jacob realized, were armed with pistols. Now they were aiming them at the crowd. They shouted that they'd shoot anyone who tried to stop them.

Jacob watched this all with wonderment. Now he understood. There had been rumors that Lord Dunmore, the King's Governor of Virginia, was going to take the gunpowder away from the townspeople. That's why they'd been guarding the Armory. It hadn't been guarded this night, though, and the rumors were true. Lord Dunmore had taken the gunpowder away from the town.

chapter 2

For Amanda and Amelia, it was just another morning. They lived in the countryside a few miles outside of Williamsburg, and the news hadn't yet traveled that far.

Amanda and Amelia were sisters. They'd been separated when they were very young. They'd only just found each other, not even two years ago.

When their original mother died, they were like orphans. Their father couldn't take care of them. He was a sailor who was always away at sea.

So the court had given them to other people to raise. The way it worked, they were sort of like apprentices. They were supposed to work in return for a place to stay, and learn how to make a living. When they were twenty-one, they'd be on their own. That's how the law worked.

Amelia's life had started out that way. She'd been given to Mr. and Mrs. Brown. She'd moved with them to Fredericksburg. They were nice to her, but she was like a servant. She helped them take care of their house and their store. Then, when they couldn't keep her anymore, she'd come back to Williamsburg.

Then she'd been given to Mr. and Mrs. Pryor. Mr. Pryor was a cruel and terrible man. He was mean to everyone, and most of all he was mean to Amanda. Her life was a misery.

Amanda had a very different fate. She'd been given to Mr. and Mrs. Lambertson. They had no children and they'd always wanted a daughter. They didn't treat her like an orphan or an apprentice at all. For years, she thought that she really was their daughter.

Then she learned that she wasn't their daughter at all, and that she had another family, long before. She searched and searched to learn who and where they were. She finally found Amelia, and then she found her sailor father. He'd agreed that Mr. and Mrs. Lambertson could adopt Amanda and Amelia too.

So now they were together again, with a new mother and a second father who loved them very much. They lived in a red brick house in the countryside. It had two floors, and their bedroom was upstairs. They had a big four-poster bed, with bed curtains all around it that you could close to keep out the cold.

They didn't keep the fire going in the night, so in winter they'd close the bed curtains tightly to  stay warm. Now it was April, but a little chilly still. They were snuggled deep under their coverlet and they didn't want to get up at all.

"Wake up, you two!" their mother called up the stairs. "You'd better get dressed and eat breakfast if you want your father to take you into Williamsburg."

Williamsburg was the capital of Virginia. The Governor and the House of Burgesses were there, and the law courts for Virginia and also the town. Mr. Lambertson was a lawyer, so he had an office there.

When he had to meet a client or when he had a case in court, he'd ride into town. Sometimes he'd take them too, in a horse-drawn carriage that was just big enough for them all.

The girls were still lazing in bed when the wonderful scent of French toast and bacon wafted up the stairs. Amelia jumped out of bed, feeling suddenly very hungry. Amanda pulled up the coverlet and put a pillow over her head. It was so cozy in bed that she didn't want to leave it.

Amelia went over to Amanda's side of the bed and pulled off the covers.

"Get up, Amanda, get up! Didn't you hear what mother said? Don't you want to go to town today?" Amelia still found it odd to say "mother" and "father," but also wonderful. She'd wanted a family so badly, for so long.

Amanda made a face at her sister but she quickly got up too. They slipped into their shifts and stockings and helped each other lace their stays. Then they put on their wrapping gowns and headed down the stairs. They'd put on their nicest silk gowns after breakfast, to go to town.

When they got to the table, their father had already finished eating. He put down the paper he was reading, pulled out his pocket watch, and looked at it.

"When you finish your breakfast, you'd better get ready, girls. I'm leaving in an hour. I'll meet you outside."

chapter 3

r. Lambertson dropped Amelia and Amanda off Duke of Gloucester Street, the main street in Williamsburg. Then he went on around the corner to his office. He had meetings all morning, he told them, but he was going back to the

house in the afternoon. Before they all left, he'd treat them to a meal at the Raleigh Tavern. He said to meet him there at noon exactly.

Amanda had checked her watch, to make sure it had the same time as her father's. It was a dainty little watch on a silver chain and she wore it like a necklace. She loved it, but it didn't always keep the right time. Sometimes it ran a little slow and sometimes she forgot to wind it.

"Where shall we go first?" Amanda asked, once their father had gone on. "Should we go to the millinery or to the apothecary?"

It really didn't matter very much. They had errands at both places and they had enough time. Amelia usually liked to go to the apothecary first, because Jacob was an apprentice there. He was her best and longest-time friend, ever since they'd met in Fredericksburg. Then he'd come to Williamsburg to be an apprentice for Doctor Galt. Now he was Amanda's friend too.

On the other hand, Amelia was eager to go to millinery. She needed to get some new ribbon. She'd worn her favorite hat so much and so long, that she needed to replace the ribbon that tied it on. She needed to sew on a new tie, and change the trim to match.

Amelia was debating which to choose, when they saw their friend Penney. She was hurrying along the sidewalk across the street.

"Penney!" Amanda called out, and they crossed over to Penney's side, taking care to avoid the horses, carriages, and carts.

All three girls had known each other for a long time. Penney had worked for Mr. Pryor too. He'd told Penney she was enslaved, even though he knew she wasn't. That's how evil a man he was. She'd been born free but she didn't know it. She'd only just discovered the truth. Luckily, she could prove it too. She worked for the Wythe family as a servant now. She still worked hard, but now she got paid and she was free to stay or leave.

"It's good to see you, but I can't talk long," Penney greeted them. "I'm running an errand and I have to get back as fast as I can. If you can, you've got to go see Josephine. She needs cheering up."

"What's wrong?" Amelia asked, suddenly very worried. Josephine had been the cook when she worked for Mr. Pryor. She'd saved her from the worst of Mr. Pryor's punishments many times.

"Has something happened to Josephine?" Amanda chimed in.

"I can't go into it now," Penney said hurriedly. "It's a complicated story and I really have to go. Also, I don't want to talk about it here in public. You'd better just go see her if you can. Maybe she'll tell you."

Penney gave a little goodbye curtsy and quickly went on her way.

The sisters just stood there, thinking of all the things that could be wrong. Was Josephine ill? Had she had an accident? They hardly dared imagine the worst thing of all — were the Robinsons going to sell her?

Josephine was enslaved, though she'd been lucky compared to some. The Robinsons were Baptists. They believed all people were equal in God's eyes, but still there was nothing they could do about slavery. Under the law in Virginia, only the government could set someone free.

The law also said that Josephine was their property, and she was valuable on account of her skills. If they had some big debt and didn't have the money to pay, they'd probably have to sell her. To Amanda and Amelia, it seemed so very wrong. How could people be bought and sold?

Amelia started to panic. All her old fears came back to her in a rush. Before the Lambertsons, Josephine was the closest to family that she'd ever known. What if she was sold to someone like Mr. Pryor, someone who'd beat her? What if she was dying from some terrible disease?

Amanda saw that her sister was so terrified, she was shaking and breathing fast. She put her arm around Amelia's shoulder.

"It's no good just wondering," she consoled her. "Maybe it's not as bad as it seems. We just have to go see her and find out what's wrong."

Amelia took a deep breath and tried to steady herself.

"Yes, we have to see her, to see how she is." Her voice was still shaky. "But what if she doesn't want to tell us?"

"We'll go to the apothecary first then," Amanda said firmly, setting off in that direction. "Maybe Jacob knows what's wrong."

chapter 4

When they opened the apothecary door, Doctor Galt smiled at them in welcome. They visited the apothecary whenever they were in town.

Most often they went to see Jacob. Sometimes they had a shopping list too. Plus, even without a list and when Jacob wasn't there, they really just liked the store.

Amelia liked it because she was interested in medicine. She'd been studying diseases and

treatments. Doctor Galt helped to teach her, even when she worked for Mr. Pryor. Even though she couldn't be a doctor, because she was a girl.

"Who knows," he'd said, "maybe you'll have a family. Then you'll know how to take care of them. Or maybe you'll have a husband who's a doctor." Women couldn't be doctors on their own, but they could help their husbands. Sometimes, if the husband died, a widow would carry on his business by herself.

Amanda wasn't that interested in medicine. She wanted to learn about the courts and the law. They'd turned out to be so important in her life that she wanted to know more about how it all worked. Even so, the apothecary seemed magical to her. It was full of strange and wonderful things. There were medicines with exotic names, like Jesuit's bark, Peruvian Balsam, and Daffy's Magic Elixir. There were good-smelling herbs and spices, like nutmeg, vanilla, cinnamon, and rosemary. There was powder to clean your teeth, chamomile flowers for tea, and all sorts of ointments and plasters. And, to top it off, there was candy.

Sometimes, when he was in a good mood, Doctor Galt would give them little presents — maybe some sugar rock candy, or some peppermints or candied almonds, or even a little bag of lavender to help them sleep.

Today they wanted to see Jacob, of course, but they also had a shopping list from their mother.

"Good morning, Doctor Galt," Amelia greeted him politely. "Is Jacob here?" She looked around, disappointed that she couldn't see him. Sometimes he was busy in the back office. When he heard their voices, though, he'd usually come out front.

Doctor Galt smiled reassuringly.

"Jacob's running an errand just now. He should be back soon. In the meantime, can I help you?"

Amelia pulled a little piece of paper from her pocket. She handed it to Doctor Galt.

"Mother gave me this list. She said she hopes that you have it all."

Doctor Galt adjusted his glasses to look at the list more closely.

"Hmmm. Yes, I have orange peel, chamomile, and Jesuit's bark. I'm pretty certain that I also have valerian, caraway, licorice, and Ward's Famous

Powder for the Headache. I don't have any of the pills, not ready-made. I'll have to have Jacob make some. I'll have to see about the rhubarb and spirits of hartshorn. I'm not sure that I have that much on hand. Does your mother want things right away or can she wait until I get everything together?"

"She said she could wait for whatever you don't have, but she'd like the rest today, if you don't mind."

Doctor Galt began to put together what he had, that their mother had asked for. Some things were in blue and white porcelain containers on the shelves. Others were tucked away in one of his many drawers. As they watched him, Amanda decided not to wait for Jacob. Maybe Doctor Galt knew what was wrong with Josephine.

"We ran into Penney on the way here. She said Josephine needed cheering up. Do you know what the problem is?"

Doctor Galt stopped what he was doing and turned to them.

"Yes, very wrong, I'm sorry to say." He looked very serious. "She's accused —" he hesitated, as if the next words were hard to say. "She's accused of poisoning someone."

"Poisoning!" The girls were horrified. They looked at him in disbelief.

"Yes, poisoning," he repeated. "You know she often gives people her herbal ointments and tonics to help them with different ailments."

It was a statement more than a question. Of course they knew. So did everyone in town, and even in the countryside. Josephine had even helped save their mother when she was so deathly sick with pneumonia. She'd given their mother a "strengthening tonic," as she called it, with Doctor Galt's permission.

"Well, she was treating one of the servants at the Raleigh Tavern," he went on. "It was one of the scullery maids in the kitchen. Betsey, I think her name was. It seems that Josephine gave her some sort of herbal tonic. Then Betsey got very sick and they called for me. It was all I could do to save her. Afterwards, she told everyone that Josephine's tonic had poisoned her."

"Josephine would never poison anyone!" Amelia didn't have any doubts at all. "She's always very careful. She won't even give people the dangerous things."

"That's as may be." Doctor Galt wasn't so sure, but he didn't want to argue. "The fact is, Betsey was very sick from something, and people believe her story. Some say Josephine just made a deadly mistake, and some say she deliberately poisoned the girl. As you must know from your studies," he added, looking at

Amelia, "even so-called 'safe' ingredients can be deadly if taken improperly. The girl swears that she only took what Josephine gave her."

Amelia was about to protest once again, but just then Jacob came back from his errand. Seeing their faces, he knew immediately what they were talking about.

"Tell him that it can't be Josephine's fault!" Amelia said to him immediately. "There must be something more to the story."

"I really can't say what happened," Jacob answered hesitantly. "The maid wasn't in such good shape when we saw her. I always thought Josephine knew what she was doing, but everyone makes mistakes."

Jacob's hesitation made Amelia angry.

"Not Josephine!" she insisted. "Josephine would never make a mistake like that. She'd never poison someone on purpose, either. She never even poisoned Mr. Pryor, when she cooked for him. And he deserved it if anyone did."

Amelia looked to Amanda for support this time, and her sister did better than Jacob.

"Amelia's right," she agreed right away. "She's been doing this for years and years and years. There's never been a problem before. Something's wrong with this maid Betsey's story. It can't have been what she said."

Doctor Galt looked unhappy. He really didn't know what to make of things. He'd thought Josephine was careful too, but how did he know?

"I hope you're right," he told them, "but whether it's true or not, people believe it. It's all over town. They're even talking about charging Josephine with attempted murder. You know she's not supposed to be treating people, being enslaved. Under the law, the consequences could be very serious for her. I could even get in trouble myself, for letting her give things to my patients."

Amelia's and Amanda's eyes met. Each knew exactly what the other was thinking. Then they looked at Jacob. It was a challenge, and after a moment, he nodded too.

Nothing was said, but they all knew what they had to do. Josephine didn't poison the maid. There must be some other explanation. They had to find out what it was.

chapter 5

Amelia and Amanda went straight from the apothecary to see Josephine. As usual, she was working away in the Robinsons' kitchen. Like most kitchens they'd seen, it was separate from the house. It was a tiny house by itself, actually. There were two stories, so Josephine had a bedroom upstairs. The kitchen was downstairs, with lots of equipment and space to cook. There were two big worktables and big windows to let the light in. There was a large fireplace with a swinging arm to hold pots over the fire and lots of shelves on the wall.

When they got there, Josephine was at one of the worktables, rolling out a pie crust. When she saw the girls she smiled, but it was a sad kind of smile that

didn't reach her eyes. She was glad to see them, but underneath it all she wasn't happy. It was easy to see.

"What are you standing in the doorway for, then?" She greeted them in her usual blunt manner. "You'd better come in so I can see you."

Amelia led the way and Amanda followed behind. They had no idea what to say to her, now that they were there.

Josephine put down the rolling pin and dusted her hands off on her apron. She checked on one of the pots simmering over the fire, tasted it, and then added a bit of spice. Then she took a plate off of one of the shelves.

"I've got some nice little cakes here if you'd like them." She folded back the cloth that was covering them and held the plate out for them to see. "That is, if you don't think I'll poison you too."

"Oh, Josephine — " Amelia began, but Josephine kept right on talking.

"If people can say such things, after all I've done — after all the years they've known me!" Her voice was tight with anger and she shook her head in disbelief. "Well, I'd never have believed it. I never would. It just goes to show you."

"It's so terrible! How can anyone believe — " Amanda managed to say, but Josephine hadn't finished.

"Well, that's it. It's over." She brushed her hands, one against the other, as if brushing away the maid Betsey and what people were saying and everything. "I'll just stay in the kitchen here and cook things for Mr. and Mrs. Robinson. I'll never give anyone anything, ever again. Not ever."

Amelia opened her mouth again to speak, but Josephine gave her a look of warning.

"I said it's over," she said firmly. "Do you hear me? It's over and done. I won't talk about it anymore. And neither will either of you."

She glared at them and they said nothing. Neither of them dared say a word. Amelia knew better than to say anything. She'd seen Josephine's temper from before. Amanda was shocked into silence.

Josephine gave them each a little cake and they ate them. When the cakes were gone, Amanda dared to speak again.

"What kind are these?" she asked timidly.

Amelia caught her breath, hoping that Josephine wouldn't take her sister's question the wrong way.

"Yes, what kind are they? They're so very good," she added quickly. "They're the best I've ever tasted — aren't they, Amanda? Aren't they the best you've ever tasted?"

"Oh, yes!" Amanda agreed. "They're absolutely the very best! That's why I wondered what kind they were."

Josephine looked at them suspiciously, but her expression softened.

"You girls!" she said, shaking her head fondly. "Whatever shall I do with you? You're hopeless, the pair of you. They're called Portugal cakes, if you must know. It's a new receipt I'm trying out. It has rose water, currants, and almonds."

After that, the visit got better. Josephine gave them two more little cakes, which disappeared as quickly as the first ones. She asked about their parents, and how they were doing, and what Amanda and Amelia had been doing, since she'd seen them last. The visit turned so pleasant that the time flew by.

"You two run along now," Josephine told them, after they'd answered all her questions. "I've got to get back to work. The Robinsons are having folks to dinner. They won't want the food to be late."

Amanda looked at her watch.

"It's almost noon! We're supposed to meet father at the tavern."

"And we haven't even been to the millinery," Amelia added unhappily. "I wanted to get some ribbon."

"You'd better get going then, and walk pretty fast. You can take some cakes for your parents too. Give me one of your handkerchiefs and I'll wrap them. "

Amelia pulled hers out of her pocket and Josephine wrapped it around two more cakes. Then she gave the sisters a meaningful look.

"I know you two," she said sternly, "so I'm telling you to stay out of this. Do you understand?"

Amanda and Amelia both said yes, they understood, but they were careful how they answered the question. Yes, they understood, that was true enough, but it didn't mean they planned to stay out of it. Not at all.

chapter 6

Amanda and Amelia had been so worried about Josephine that they'd hardly noticed anything around them. Now, as they hurried back to the Raleigh Tavern, they started noticing things. Things were different somehow. Here and there, little groups of people were standing close together, talking. They seemed angry and upset. There was an atmosphere of tension. Something seemed to be wrong.

It was all so surprising that they even forgot about Josephine.

"Has something happened?" Amanda asked their father, once they were settled at a little table in a semi-private room at the Raleigh Tavern. "People seem to be upset about something."

Their father studied them for a moment, as if deciding how much to say.

"You can tell us," Amelia encouraged him. "We should know what's going on."

"All right," he agreed. "You're old enough to understand, I know. I just don't want you to worry. It may not be anything, in the end. It may all get resolved."

He paused as the waiter came up to the table. The waiter carefully set down their food, but the girls ignored it. They waited for their father to go on.

"Lord Dunmore had the British Marines take gunpowder from the Armory," he explained. "They came in secretly in the night. They probably meant to take it all away. Some of the men in town realized what was happening, though, and they stopped them before they were finished."

"But isn't it his right to take it?" Amanda was confused. "After all, he's the governor."

"That's a good question," their father said approvingly. "In fact, the gunpowder doesn't belong to the King or Parliament. It belongs to the town militia. The townspeople paid for it, so it's theirs. Lord Dunmore had no right to take it."

The girls knew about the local militia. It was the local militia who were responsible for defending the towns and countryside. The militias were like regular armies, only part-time and volunteers. They were organized and approved by the local governments. They had officers, uniforms, and rules.

There were some British soldiers in the colonies, but they were mostly on the frontier. Since the so-called "Boston Tea Party," there were British soldiers in Boston too. They weren't there to defend the people in Boston. They were there to keep them in line.

"Why did he take the gunpowder then," Amelia asked, "if it wasn't his?"

"He doesn't want us to be able to defend ourselves

against the British soldiers. He wants to have all the power, to crush things, if things go wrong."

Amelia and Amanda suddenly understood. When some people had ruined a load of tea, the British Government had punished everyone in Boston. Now Boston was like a kind of jail. There were warships blocking their port and trade, and soldiers everywhere. People were even forced to let soldiers live in their homes.

It was so high-handed and so harsh that it had made all the other colonies furious. Penney had overheard Mr. Jefferson and the others talking about it, when she worked at the Raleigh Tavern before. The Parliament thought it could treat the colonies however it liked, they said, even though they were British citizens like any others. It wasn't right and it wasn't legal, according to the British law. There'd been talk about independence, and people were talking about it more and more.

"Lord Dunmore has a hot temper." Their father said it very quietly, so only the girls could hear him. "I think he's let his temper get ahold of him. I think he's made a mistake, taking the gunpowder. This will only make things worse. Now everyone is mad. Some want to go to the Governor's Palace with weapons. They want to force him to give the gunpowder back. He'd call in the British soldiers then, and that would be a disaster. Mr. Randolph and some of the other town leaders are trying to calm things down."

The girls ate their meal in silence, absorbing this news.

Amelia found it frightening. What would happen if people actually tried to fight a war against Britain? The colonies were weak. Britain was one of the strongest countries in the world. How could they ever win such a war? And why did they think that things would get better, even if they did? In her experience, changes didn't always work out for the better. Sometimes changes only made things worse.

Amanda was worried too, but her worries went the other way. Every year, it seemed, things in the colonies got worse and worse. The Parliament never asked and never listened. They treated the colonies however they liked. They didn't care what happened to the people who lived there. They had control, and the colonists had no say.

Now Lord Dunmore was making sure that people were unable to defend themselves. Why? What was he planning to do to them? What would life be like if colonists had no rights at all? What if they were treated just like they were enslaved?

It was only when the waiter brought them all rice pudding that Amelia and Amanda remembered about Josephine.

"We never got to the millinery," Amelia began, "because we went to see Josephine. A terrible thing has happened."

"It happened right here," Amanda added. "It was a kitchen maid right here in the tavern! She said Josephine poisoned her and people believe her! Now Josephine is in terrible trouble."

Their father was very surprised by the news.

"Josephine? I can't believe it. Are you certain?"

"Yes, Doctor Galt told us, and Jacob too," Amelia answered. "Josephine won't say much about it, but she's very angry. If they decide to punish her, she could get in worse trouble too."

They finished their meal and headed for home, very somber. It was a day full of very bad news.

chapter 7

A few days afterwards, the news got worse. Amanda and Amelia were studying in the library. The Lambertsons believed that they should be well educated. A lot of parents didn't. Many thought girls only needed to know practical things, like sewing and cleaning. Maybe they would also learn how to read a little and their names, and know how to add and subtract enough for their shopping.

Mostly Mrs. Lambertson taught them and sometimes their father. Sometimes they learned from the books in the library. Their parents also hired tutors who came from time to time. One man taught them French and math, and another one taught dancing. He taught them all the latest dances, and also how to stand and move. The girls weren't very fond of the dancing master, because he was so strict. They were fond of dancing, though.

The Lambertsons had an unusually large library. There were shelves and shelves of leather-bound books. There were law books of course, since Mr. Lambertson was a lawyer. In addition there were books on all kinds of other subjects. There were books on medicine, history, and geography. There were novels, plays, poetry, and stories about travels to far-away lands.

Today, their mother was helping them with the math problems that their tutor had given them, the last time he was there. They needed to finish them because he was coming back soon.

Their father had gone to his office in Williamsburg early that morning. It was around noon when he returned. He came straight into the library. They could tell from his face that something was terribly wrong.

"What's happened?" their mother asked anxiously.

"There's been fighting in Massachusetts," he said. "Serious fighting. There was a battle between colonists and British soldiers. People were killed."

The news was so incredible that they could hardly believe their ears. Fighting? Between the people of Massachusetts and the soldiers? People killed?

"There were two battles actually," their father went on. "One was very small and the other was large. First

the British soldiers marched through a town called Lexington. There were hundreds of them, with cannons. Seventy-seven militiamen tried to stop them. Of course, they couldn't. There were so few against so many. They tried anyway, and nine of them died.

"Then the soldiers went on to a nearby town called Concord. This time, there were thousands of militiamen, they say. Amazingly, after hours of fighting, the British soldiers gave up and went away. This time, many soldiers were killed, and militiamen too."

"What started it?" Their mother was stunned by the news. She'd been worried that something like this might happen. Some of the people in Massachusetts wanted to get everyone fighting, no matter what. The

British army would never stand for it, having soldiers killed by colonists and being forced to retreat. They'd do everything in their power to strike back.

Their father looked grim.

"It was the same thing as happened here. The British authorities wanted to take away the militia's arms. Only instead of twenty or so marines and sailors coming in the middle of the night, it was seven hundred well-armed troops in the daytime. They even had cannons."

"Just think, it could have happened in Williamsburg!" Their mother was horrified by the thought. "Thank heavens that Mr. Randolph and the others are trying to calm things down."

Amelia was even more horrified than her mother was. How could the people in Massachusetts shoot at the soldiers? Britain was their country too. It was their own King they were fighting, their own soldiers!

That was the end of the math problems. Their mother tried to go on for a while, but she couldn't concentrate. She told the girls to "study something" and left the room.

"What's wrong with those people in Massachusetts?" Amelia asked her sister once their mother had gone. "How can they rebel against their own King and country?"

"He hasn't been acting very much like he's their King, is why." Amanda was upset by the news also, but she understood better than her sister why people were so unhappy with British rule. "They're not treating us like we're part of Britain. Remember what Mr. Jefferson and the others said when the British punished Boston for the Tea Party. They punished everyone in the entire city, even though only a few people destroyed the tea. They treated everyone in Boston like they were an enemy. They'd never do that in Britain. The way they're treating us isn't right or fair."

Amelia frowned.

"Things aren't always fair. That isn't an excuse for treason. Anyway, it's just about money, is what I think. The people in Boston are greedy. They want the British Government to support them and defend them, but they don't want to pay anything for it, not even a little bit. They want to take but they don't want to give anything back."

Just then, their mother came to the door and looked in.

"Are you two studying? It doesn't look like you're studying."

"Yes, Mother," they chorused, and they gave up their argument, at least for the time being.

Amanda pulled out a book from the shelf. It was an adventure story, but in French. Reading a book in

French counted as "studying," she told herself, even though it was an adventure story.

Amelia went over and got *The London Dispensatory*. This was the same book Doctor Galt had given her, months and months ago. It had information about all the different medicines and herbs. She'd been working for Mr. Pryor then and she had to study in secret. He'd tried to burn the book when he caught her reading it, late at night by the fire.

The two of them read quietly for nearly an hour. Then their mother called them to dinner.

Amelia looked up from her book and rubbed her eyes. The print was very small and the light in the room was fading.

"So what have you learned?" Amanda asked her.

"All I've learned," Amelia said wearily, "is that it's going to be harder to figure out what happened than I thought it would be. There are a lot of herbs and other medicines that can be very bad, if you take them wrong. I should have asked more questions, like what Josephine gave her and what the symptoms were."

Amanda was sorry too.

"It's too bad we didn't, but it's not surprising. We were so shocked that Josephine could be accused of poisoning anyone. It drove everything else from our minds."

"I don't suppose Josephine will tell me anything," Amelia predicted, remembering how Josephine had told them to stay out of it. "If I even asked her, I bet she'd get mad. I guess I'll just have to wait until we see Doctor Galt and Jacob again."

Amelia set her list aside. They both went back to doing math problems, until dinner time came around.

It was a strange, silent dinner. No one said a word. The food was especially lovely, with roast beef, fried potatoes, and almond pudding for dessert. Their parents hardly even seemed to taste the food. After dinner, they went off to Mr. Lambertson's office and shut the door. They spent a long time together in there, talking. They still seemed worried and distracted when they came to kiss the girls goodnight.

chapter 8

When Amanda and Amelia came down to breakfast the next morning, things seemed almost back to normal. Their father looked up at them from his paper as usual, and their mother greeted them with a smile.

Halfway through the meal, Amelia looked at Amanda with a question in her eyes. Amanda understood her immediately. Their father was likely going into Williamsburg today, to get more news. Should they ask if they could go with him? This could be the only chance to go ask Jacob and Doctor Galt more questions for quite a while. Once their tutor came, they'd have to stay home for as long as he was there.

While they hesitated, there was a knock at the front door. Their father quickly got up to answer it. Soon the girls heard a familiar voice in the hall.

"Good morning! I've brought the spirits of hartshorn and the pills."

The girls smiled at their luck. It was Jacob! Now they didn't have to go to town.

"Doctor Galt thought maybe you needed these as soon as possible," he explained to Mrs. Lambertson, as he came into the dining room. "I'm glad he sent me, I have to say. It's different, now that Doctor Pasteur is there. I'm not used to it. It was nice to get away."

Mrs. Lambertson frowned.

"Doctor Pasteur seems a very fine doctor," she chided Jacob gently. "This partnership will be good for Doctor Galt."

"Oh yes, Doctor Pasteur is very fine," Jacob said quickly. "I don't doubt it at all. The problem is, there are two of them and just one of me. Doctor Galt tells me one thing, and then Doctor Pasteur tells me another. Or Doctor Pasteur says something on his way out the door, and I don't understand what he's saying. It's all so different." He sighed. "I suppose I'll get used to it in time."

"Well, thank you for coming," Mrs. Lambertson said kindly. "You left early and you must be hungry. Why don't you stay a while and have some breakfast?

Mr. Lambertson and I have work to do, but I'm sure the girls will be happy to keep you company."

Jacob sat down gladly. He was hungry, that was true.

As soon as they were alone together, Amelia began to question him.

"I'm so glad you came. I've been thinking about what happened with the maid — what really happened, I mean, not what she says. I've been studying what might have caused her symptoms and I realize that I need to know more."

Jacob looked longingly at the food on the table. There was bread and butter, sausages and little meat pies, and hardboiled egg too. It all looked very good.

"Can I eat my breakfast first?"

Reluctantly, Amelia agreed.

Jacob didn't hurry, despite how impatient the girls obviously were. He ate every last bite, and a second helping of sausages too.

"All right, then," he said, when he finally laid down his fork. "Go ahead and ask your questions."

"I have four questions, to begin with," Amelia began again. As she spoke, she ticked the questions off on her fingers, one by one. "First, what was wrong with the maid, that she wanted something from Josephine? Second, what did Josephine give her? Third, what were the maid's symptoms, that Doctor Galt said that she'd been poisoned? And fourth, what did you do to save her?"

"That's an awful lot of questions," Jacob said teasingly. "Maybe I'd better have more breakfast first."

The girls just glared at him.

"Oh, all right," he said, smiling back at them. "Don't get into such a fuss. I don't know all the answers, but I'll tell you what I can."

He closed his eyes, trying to remember all the details. Then he took a deep breath and answered what he could.

"First, I don't know what the maid's problem was. I don't know what Josephine gave her, either. I'll ask

Doctor Galt, but I don't think he knows more than I do. They only called us in afterwards, when she was already in a bad way.

"According to one of the cooks there, she said she felt sick, and then she threw up some. She said her stomach hurt a lot, like there was a knife stuck into her. When it didn't go away, and got worse even, they came to get Doctor Galt. By the time we got there, she was having seizures. We couldn't really ask her questions. She was only moaning and crying.

"Doctor Galt said it had to be poison, for symptoms like that to come on so fast. So he gave her something to make her throw up, in case any poison was left in her stomach."

"What did he give her?" Amelia asked. "I'm just curious."

"I think it was just Ipecac syrup, the usual thing. He also gave her sugar water with egg whites beaten in, to dilute the poison, followed by marshmallow tea. He couldn't give her any kind of antidote, since no one knew what the poison was. He prescribed chamomile tea for the seizures, and laudanum for the pain. It was a couple of days before she really recovered. Then she said Josephine's tonic was to blame."

"You know that couldn't be true," Amanda said firmly.

"It doesn't sound very likely, I suppose." Jacob still didn't sound convinced. "But like Doctor Galt says, everyone makes mistakes — "

"Not Josephine! She never makes mistakes." Amelia gave Jacob a hard look, daring him to disagree with her.

Amanda was equally positive.

"She's never ever made a mistake before."

Jacob looked from one to the other, and then gave in.

"I guess you're right."

Both girls smiled at him.

"Of course we are."

"So if it wasn't the tonic," Amanda concluded, "she must have taken something else. We only need to find out what it was."

To say it like that, it sounded so easy. But it wasn't. It was hard.

chapter 9

News didn't take long to spread around Williamsburg. Soon everyone had heard about the fighting at Lexington and Concord. The news wasn't always accurate, but people understood the most important part. There had been a serious battle between the British soldiers and the colonists in Massachusetts. Both soldiers and colonists had died.

Amanda and Amelia weren't the only ones with different views about who was to blame for the fighting. Arguments were going on all over Virginia and other colonies too. Were the colonists to blame, or the Parliament and the King? Most people were on the colonists' side.

For Penney, the day had been an especially busy one. Mr. and Mrs. Wythe were going to be entertaining a group of important gentlemen for dinner. There was a lot of shopping and cleaning and setting up to do. After she'd finished her morning tasks, she went to find Lydia Broadnax, the housekeeper, to find out what she should do next.

Penney found the housekeeper in the dining room, talking with the coachman — arguing, more like.

"I suppose you've heard about those people in Massachusetts?" she was saying. "It's just like what happened here, only worse."

"So what? It's nothing to do with us," the man said sourly. "Whatever happens, we're still enslaved."

Lydia gave him a sharp-eyed look.

"Don't you be too sure. When big things happen — really big things like this — it affects everyone. It matters, whether for better or for worse."

"*If* anything happens," the coachman replied stubbornly. "For years now, it's been the same. Something happens, and then some of the white people get upset for a while, and then things calm down again." He nodded for emphasis, but then he looked at them thoughtfully.

"There's a rumor though, that's pretty interesting." He lowered his voice to where it was almost a whisper. "They say Lord Dunmore would free any slaves who fight with the British against the colonists. If the rumor's true, I'd have to think long and hard what to do, I can tell you."

Then he shook his head.

"Probably nothing to it, though. Even if the rumor's true, there won't be fighting. What's happening now is like a summer storm. It comes on strong, but just as fast it disappears. Just you wait. You'll see I'm right about it."

Having delivered himself of his final words, he turned away and left them.

Lydia shook her head and turned to Penney.

"He's got his head in the sand, poor fellow. Whatever you think of it, in times like these, it's important to know what's going on."

"And what do you think, Miss Broadnax?" The voice belonged to Edith Cumbo, a cheerful woman with an ample figure. Like Penney, she'd been born free. Now she supported herself as a laundress and seamstress. She'd just come by to deliver some laundry and she'd heard the last bit of Lydia's conversation.

"I haven't decided," Lydia said carefully, "but I'm leaning towards being what people call a 'patriot.' More and more, it seems, the British over there in London don't care for the people in Virginia. For them, we're just a place for them to make money and get rich, like India and Jamaica and their other colonies. Like it or not, our lives depend on the white people here in the colonies. If things get bad for them, we'll suffer even more than we do know now."

"What about you, Miss Cumbo?" Penney asked the laundress. She hadn't made up her own mind and she was curious to know what others thought.

The laundress considered it.

"I have to tell you, that's a hard question. From what I can see, the white people here in Virginia are bound to keep black people enslaved. I've heard things are better over there in Britain. On the other hand, the way things are going, I'm thinking the people who stay loyal to the King won't be too popular here. It might be better in Britain, but I can't pick up and move like some people. My whole life is here."

Penney nodded.

"That makes a lot of sense. Can I ask another question? Of both of you? It's about something else."

"Go on," Lydia told her. "You just ask, and we'll decide if we'll answer."

"It's about that maid Betsey, the one who says that Josephine poisoned her. I've known Josephine for as long as I can remember. I just can't see how she'd ever poison anyone. Not by mistake and certainly not on purpose."

Lydia and Edith shared a look of understanding. It seemed to Penney that they'd talked about this before, and they both thought the same.

"We think that's very likely true, what you say," Lydia said for both of them. "It's a shame for Josephine, but it seems that Betsey's got everyone believing her. The people that matter, anyway."

"Then what do you think really happened?"

"Are they looking into things, these friends of yours?" Lydia guessed rightly. "Is it like Mr. Jefferson's violin, all over again?"

"Is that so bad?" Penney said defensively. "They did find the one who really took it, didn't they?"

"Yes, I suppose so," Lydia allowed. "They had a lot of help though."

Penney smiled at her.

"That's just it! We need to help them. And you too," she added, turning to Miss Cumbo. "You get around more than we do, and you hear things. Between the laundry and the sewing, you must get to half the houses in Williamsburg."

"Half the houses, maybe even more," the laundress agreed, but she didn't look very enthusiastic.

"I'll try to help, for Josephine's sake," Lydia said willingly. "I'm on pretty good terms with one of the cooks there at the Raleigh Tavern. If I happen to see him, I could ask some questions. You know most of the servants there," she added, speaking to Penney, "since you used to work there. So you can ask too."

chapter 10

What had the maid Betsey taken that made her so ill? Amelia figured that it was up to her and Jacob to figure it out. After all, they were the ones who'd been studying medicine, and that's what it was all about. She started spending her free time in the library by herself, looking at books like *The London Dispensatory* and *The British Herbal.* She was making a list of everything that could cause the symptoms that Jacob said Betsey had.

At first, Amanda read quietly in the corner while Amelia worked on her list. From time to time, she'd look up and smile at her sister, but Amelia was too busy to notice. Amanda was starting to feel left out.

"What are you doing?" she asked finally. "Can I help you?"

Amelia shook her head.

"Thanks, but I don't think so. It's all about herbs and medicine, and you don't know about those things. I've been studying them and you haven't."

"It's all in the book, right?" Amanda said it a bit sharply. She knew Amelia didn't mean to hurt her feelings, but she had. "You're just reading what it says there, looking for words like 'nausea,' right? Well, I can read too, so I can do that as well as you."

At first, Amelia didn't understand why Amanda sounded so unhappy. Then she realized that Amanda had a point.

"Yes, I guess so," she agreed. "There's no point to us both doing it, though. We'd both of us be doing the exact same thing."

Amanda sighed, but she didn't argue. She knew it was true. She left her sister alone in the library, making her list.

It was a lovely spring day, so Amanda went out to the garden. She loved the garden, and often went out to help the gardener, John. He felt like family to her, like an uncle perhaps. She could tell him things that she didn't want to tell her parents, and he'd give her good advice. He always seemed to understand her and guess her moods.

When she went to the garden, she could see that John was very busy. At this time of year there was a lot to be done. After the long winter's rest, things were coming to life again. Seeds had to be sown and the ground prepared for them. Tender

young plants from the greenhouse had to be moved outside. Most of all, there was weeding.

The weeds grew fast. They grew faster than everything else in the garden. They'd crowd out everything else if they could. They were creeping over the strawberries. They were towering over the tender new seedlings. They were spreading through the dirt in between. Chickweed, dandelion, and other unwanted visitors seemed to be everywhere.

"They always grow better than other things, and where you don't want them," he always said. "That's why they call them weeds."

Today, as they worked together, he looked at her from time to time. It was as if he knew there was something on her mind, but he didn't want to ask.

She wanted to tell him, but she didn't want to bother him when he was so busy. Then too, there were too many things in her mind. They were all so tangled together, that she didn't know where to start.

She was worried about Josephine, of course. She was worried about whether there might be fighting here in Virginia, like there was in Massachusetts. Most of all, she felt lonely. With her sister all wrapped up in making her list, the way she was, it was like she was an only child again. She hadn't minded so much then, because it was all she knew. Now she had a sister, though, it was different. Amelia wasn't just her sister, she was also her best friend. Without her sister's company, the days suddenly seemed very long.

After a while it turned colder, so Amanda went back inside. She was making a sampler, in order to practice her stitches. She'd already made a sketch of the design. First there would be the whole alphabet, in tiny cross stitches. Then, under that, there would be all the numbers from one to ten, along with her name and the date. Then, around it, she'd make a colorful border of fancy embroidery, with birds and vines and flowers.

She couldn't keep her mind on the sewing, though. She kept thinking about Josephine, and Amelia, and her list. Finally, she gave up sewing. She wasn't doing a very good job anyway, with her mind on other things. She put down the sampler and went off to the library.

Amelia was still there, hunched over in their father's chair. She was going through *A Curious Herbal*, with her list on the table beside her. It was like she hadn't moved at all for days.

Amanda went over and picked up the list off the table. As she'd suspected, it was way too long. It filled one whole piece of paper and most of the other side.

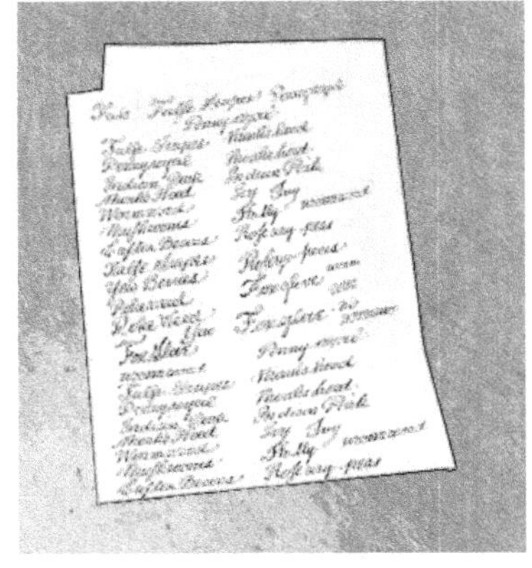

"I've been thinking." She said it loudly, to get her sister's attention. Then she waited until Amelia stopped and looked up from the book.

"It seems to me," Amanda continued, "that your book has practically every herb and medicine in the world. Isn't that right?"

"Yes, I expect so," Amelia answered, puzzled by the question. "It's a reference book about all the medicinal herbs and things, so that's how it's supposed to be."

Amanda nodded.

"Just as I thought. It's got practically everything in the world. Probably some of them are very rare and expensive too."

"Yes, of course."

"So I don't think Betsey could get all those things that are in the book," Amanda concluded. "Maybe you couldn't even get them in London. We don't really need to worry about all those things. Whatever she took, it had to be something she could get here in Williamsburg. Isn't that right?"

Amelia looked at the list unhappily. She understood what her sister was saying, but she'd spent so much time on it!

"It's just a beginning," she defended herself. "It's important to start with everything, so I wouldn't leave anything out."

Amelia looked back at her book.

"Anyway, I'm almost done." She picked up the book to show Amanda how far she'd gotten. Sure enough, there were only a few pages left.

Amanda felt her spirits lift. She had her sister back again!

"That's great," she said happily. "Now that we've got the list, though, we need to make it a whole lot smaller. We need to know what things you can get in Williamsburg. We need to ask Jacob and Doctor Galt."

chapter **11**

Amanda and Amelia were anxious to get into town as soon as possible, but it was impossible. They were stuck at home now. The tutor had finally arrived.

The tutor traveled from house to house, and when he came, he stayed for days. First he had them go over the math problems he'd left them. Then he gave them more problems to do. Then he tutored them in French. Then he tested them on history and grammar. He even threw in a little dancing practice, though he wasn't even their dancing master. He kept them so busy that they had time for little else.

Finally, he left. Now they could go to town again!

This time they rode their horses in, just the two of them. They each had a horse of their very own. Amelia's horse was a white mare named Belle. Amanda's horse was a bay-colored thoroughbred named Mallory. Both Amanda and Amelia were good riders. Amanda had been riding longer, but Amelia had a way with horses that was special. For her, even the wildest horses obeyed.

When they got to Williamsburg, they went first to their aunt and uncle's house. It was a white house with a white picket fence around it, on the edge of town. The Taylors were actually distant cousins. They were as old as their parents, though, so the girls called them "Aunt Sarah" and "Uncle John."

Their aunt was always pleased to see them. Usually she offered them something good to eat, thinking they'd be hungry after the ride. Today it was fresh-baked apple cake, with sweet cider to wash it down. They chatted with their aunt while they ate the cake. Then they set off for the apothecary to see Jacob.

Things felt a lot calmer than the last time they were there, right after the gunpowder was taken. It wasn't normal, though. Not at all. Up and down Duke of Gloucester Street, Amelia and Amanda saw strange men wearing hunting shirts, big, loose shirts with fringed capes at the shoulder. Many were carrying tomahawks or guns. Some were by the Armory—a few had even set up tents there—and some were wandering around.

When the girls got to the apothecary, there were two inside as customers, in addition to regular customers from the town.

Neither Doctor Galt nor Doctor Pasteur was there, so Jacob had to take care of everyone. The girls waited patiently in the corner until he'd taken care of everyone and they were alone.

"Who are all these men?" Amelia asked anxiously. "What are they doing here? I thought things had settled down."

"They're militia, of course." Jacob thought it was obvious. All these men in the hunting shirt uniforms — who else would they be? It was equally obvious, he thought, what they were doing in Williamsburg. "They're here to defend us against the British soldiers."

Amelia frowned.

"I don't like it, all those men with weapons. Some of them look like troublemakers. They seem dangerous to me."

"Not at all," Jacob dismissed her worries. "They're here to defend us, not to cause trouble. I'll be one of them. I'm going to join the militia myself."

Amanda snorted in disbelief.

"You? You're not sixteen. You've got to be sixteen to be in the militia."

To Jacob, that seemed like a mere technicality.

"I'll say I am. I don't know when I was born, not really. I could be sixteen. I could be just small for my age."

Amelia gave him a hard look, up and down.

"No one would ever believe you're sixteen, not ever. You'd never fool anyone. You don't look even as old as you really are."

Amelia was going to go in greater detail about why he'd never pass for sixteen, but Amanda nudged her with her elbow, rather hard.

"Give him the list! Now, before someone else comes in. Remember what we're here for."

Amelia quickly pulled her list out of her pocket.

"I made a list of all the things that could cause the symptoms Betsey had," she said, handing it over. "The symptoms you mentioned, that is. But it has to have been something that she could get here, so I crossed off some of them. Can you look at it and see what you think? What could she have gotten in Williamsburg, to make her sick like that?"

The list was still very long. Jacob spent a little time looking it over before he said anything.

"Some of these things are very common," he told them, "like pennyroyal, and Indian pink, and wormwood. Probably most of the apothecaries in Williamsburg carry them. I doubt she would have gotten these, though. Doctor Galt is very careful when he prescribes any of these or sells them. He makes sure people understand that they can be dangerous."

"There are many apothecaries in Williamsburg," Amanda pointed out. "Maybe some of them aren't as careful as you are."

Jacob thought about it for a moment, and then shook his head.

"Maybe, but Betsey's just a kitchen maid. It would be strange for her to go buying medicine for herself, without anyone's say-so. If she had, someone would probably remember it. Then, when she said she was poisoned, they would have said something."

Amelia and Amanda both looked discouraged.

"We know there are a lot of questions," Amelia admitted, "but we have to start somewhere."

"At first, we thought it would be an easy thing to find out what she took," Amanda added, "but it just seems to get harder and harder."

The girls looked so depressed that Jacob felt bad. He himself wasn't feeling very hopeful. It didn't seem likely that they'd ever find out what Betsey took, however hard they tried. He tried to think of something more cheerful.

"Have you talked to Penney? She came by the other day to pick up something for Mrs. Wythe. She said that she's trying to find out things also. She said that Lydia, the housekeeper there at the Wythe's, doesn't believe Josephine poisoned the maid either. Lydia knows one of the cooks at the Raleigh Tavern pretty well. She was going to talk to him. Maybe he knows something about what actually happened."

Amelia and Amanda cheered up at this news. There wasn't any way they could quiz the servants at the Raleigh Tavern, but Lydia and Penney could do it.

"Maybe you can talk to her?" Amelia looked at Jacob encouragingly. "We're not in town all that much, and Penney's usually busy working."

Jacob carefully folded the list and put it in his pocket.

"All right, I'll work on the list," he promised, "and I'll try to talk to Penney. I'll talk with Doctor Galt about it too. Maybe he can check with some of the other apothecaries. I wouldn't get your hopes up, though. It's a lot to figure out, with so many apothecaries in town and so many different possibilities."

With thanks and smiles, the girls left Jacob and hurried off to Mrs. Charlton's millinery.

chapter 12

Mrs. Charlton's millinery had all the very nicest things to wear, imported from France and England. She had plain and fancy caps and hats of straw and silk and linen, fabric for every sort of jacket or gown, and ribbons and lace and other fancy trimmings. There were buckles for your shoes, earrings, necklaces, and other jewelry. She

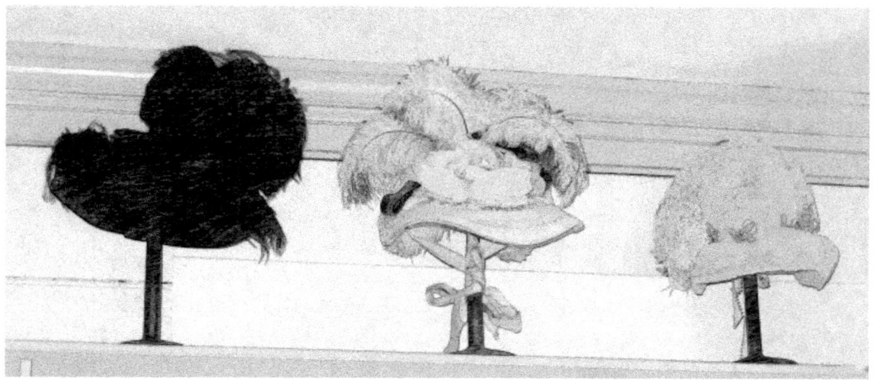

had mittens, gloves, and muffs to keep you warm, and fans to cool you.

When they entered the shop, Mrs. Charlton was talking to another customer.

"Lord Dunmore was quite right to take the gunpowder," she was saying. "Otherwise, who knows what these hotheads here might do. This talk about independence is just plain treason, if you ask me."

Amanda frowned at Mrs. Charlton's words. She didn't think Mr. Jefferson, Mr. Washington, and the others were hotheads. And was it treason, to want what was yours? Hadn't her father said the gunpowder belonged to the town, not to Lord Dunmore? Is it treason to want to be treated fairly?

Amelia, however, was listening with approval to every word. Mrs. Charlton was saying exactly what she was thinking.

Seeing them, Mrs. Charlton broke off her conversation and turned to greet them with a smile.

"Amanda, Amelia, how good to see you. May I show you anything?"

"We're looking for ribbons, if you please."

Mrs. Charlton pulled out a tray of ribbons from one of the drawers. She set the tray down on the counter for Amelia to look at. As Amelia studied them one by one, the milliner went back to her conversation.

"That Mr. Henry is the worst," she went on. "He wants war with the British so badly that he's willing to be the one to cause it. Did you hear what he did in Yorktown? He almost caused the British warship to fire its cannons on the town. The way I hear it, he did this entirely on his own, without any approval or or-

ders from anyone. He'll get some poor innocent souls killed some day. Mark my words," she added earnestly, "men like him are dangerous."

Amelia took a long time looking at the ribbons, because she was listening to Mrs. Charlton. Amanda was growing more and more impatient.

"Will you make up your mind," she hissed. "We haven't got all day. We have to go back home again."

Amelia wanted to keep listening, but she complied. She picked out one ribbon from the lot and went over to Mrs. Charlton.

"Mrs. Charlton, please, I like this one."

Mrs. Charlton took the ribbon and examined it. It was silk, about an inch wide. It had tiny pink flowers embroidered down the center, and a gold and green border on either side.

"Yes, this one is special. It came from France. How much do you need of it?"

"I should have six yards, I think. That should be enough for the hat tie and trim, don't you think?"

Mrs. Charlton checked back in the drawer.

"I'm sorry but I haven't got that much right now. I'm expecting to get more very soon. Can you come back next week? I should have it by then."

Amelia went over to the ribbons and picked out a second one. It was plainer, just pink silk, with strips of gold along the edges.

"What about this one?"

Mrs. Charlton took it and checked in one of her drawers.

"Yes, there's enough of that one, if you'd like that instead."

Amelia tried to decide. The second one was nice, but the first one was so much nicer.

"I really like the first one best," she said finally. "If you get it, could you set six yards aside for me? If it doesn't come, I'll take the second one."

"All right," Mrs. Charlton agreed. "Come back in a week or so."

Having done what they needed to do, the girls said goodbye to their aunt, and then they rode home again.

chapter 13

Meanwhile, Penney had learned quite a lot. Lydia had gone to the Raleigh Tavern to pick up a walking stick that Mr. Wythe had left there. While she was there, she went to talk to her friend Ned. He was one of the cooks at the tavern.

"You know Penney," Lydia began. "The girl who used to work here."

"Yes of course." Ned smiled. "I miss having her around. She was always so pleasant and so cheerful. Not like some," he added, casting a dark look in the direction of a scullery maid.

The maid had her back to them, so Lydia couldn't see who it was. From Ned's comment, though, Lydia guessed that this was Betsey, the maid who said Josephine poisoned her. This wasn't the time or place,

she realized, to ask about her. Not with Betsey herself listening in.

Lydia quickly came up with a different strategy.

"I think Penney misses you too. She said you were always kind to her. I know you're busy here, but maybe she could come by some time to say hello?"

As she said it, Lydia looked pointedly at the scullery maid, whose back was still turned. Then she whispered "about Josephine." She said it so softly that even her friend could barely hear, but he understood her meaning.

"That would be nice. I'm not so busy this Sunday. Maybe after church, if she's free then?"

"Yes, after church sounds fine," Lydia agreed. "I'll tell her she can come by."

Come Sunday after church, Penney went straight to the Raleigh Tavern kitchen. Knowing she was coming,

Ned had arranged it so he could leave the kitchen for a little while, to talk to her without anyone listening in.

"You're here on account of Josephine?" he asked, once they were alone together.

Penney understood that he couldn't take much time away from the cooking. She went straight to the point.

"We all — Amanda, Amelia, Jacob, and I — we don't believe she could have poisoned anyone. She's never made a mistake like that, not in all the years I've known her. So we're wondering, what is Betsey like? Why would she say that Josephine poisoned her?"

"I wasn't there at the time, sorry to say." Ned wanted to be helpful. He liked Josephine too. "They'd hired me out for a week, to cook at a plantation out of town. So I can't give you details about that. I can tell you about Betsey, though. To be blunt, she's a silly girl, and not too bright. She's not too honest either. The way I figure it is, she needed someone to blame, so she picked Josephine. She's like that. It wouldn't be the first time she's blamed someone else for something she did herself.

"She dropped a day full of dishes one time," Ned went on. "There was broken crockery and food all over. She said one of the waiters bumped into her and hit her arm. He got into trouble before he could say a word to defend himself. Afterwards, he swore to me he didn't touch her. I know her and I know him, and I believe him."

"If that's the way she is," Penney asked curiously, "why did people believe her when she blamed Josephine?"

"Only some of us have spent enough time with her to know how she really is. With the Southalls, she always got away with it. She's a pretty girl and she can look ever-so-innocent. She's full of smiles and flattery too. If you didn't know her well, you'd believe her. That waiter I mentioned, he tried to say what really happened, but they thought he was just trying to shift the blame. It seems like, if you say anything against her, you'd be the one getting in trouble, not her. So people stopped saying things after a while."

Penney understood. It was a familiar story, sad to say. She'd met people like Betsey before.

Little by little, when she could catch them, Penney talked to others at the tavern too. She still knew most of them, and most of them liked her. The staff hadn't changed much since she left to work for the Wythe's. Finding the time to talk to them wasn't easy, though. She was busy and they were busy too. Morning to night, the tavern was a busy place. It not only served food and drink at all hours, but there were overnight guests in addition. You had to work long and hard to keep up with things, whether you were enslaved, indentured, or hired.

Everything Penney learned confirmed what Ned had told her. It seemed clear that Betsey had blamed Josephine for something she'd done to herself. The next question was, what exactly had she done?

chapter 14

"Things will calm down again," the coachman had told Penney and Lydia. For a while, it seemed like he was right. Things did calm down, at least in Williamsburg. It didn't happen overnight.

In fact, there were some scary times. Lord Dunmore sent his family off to stay on a warship near Yorktown. It was for their safety, he said. Others said it was because he planned to have British soldiers invade the town. He was fed up with rebellious colonists, the

rumors said. The warships were planning to sail up the river to Williamsburg. Then they'd "subdue" the colonists by force. Williamsburg would be like Boston was. Soldiers would be everywhere, ready to lock them up or even shoot them if they did anything wrong.

For a few weeks, everyone in Yorktown and Williamsburg was afraid that the ships and soldiers were coming. They looked anxiously at the river and the roads. Even people in the countryside, like the Lambertsons, were worried. What would happen next? What happened in Boston, would it happen here?

Then, somehow it all disappeared. Lady Dunmore and the children came back to Williamsburg. The gunpowder was paid for. The tension and anger died down.

Best of all, it seemed like the British Prime Minister was finally taking the colonists seriously. They'd sent many complaints to the Parliament and King, but they'd all been ignored. Now at least someone was trying to fix things. The Parliament even adopted a plan to give the colonies more control over taxes. If the colonies agreed to it, maybe the problem would be solved!

The members of the House of Burgesses came back to town to meet again. Things were looking up. The Burgesses had barely started meeting, however, when Lord Dunmore made everyone furious, once again.

It happened just the day after Penney talked to Ned.

One of Mr. Lambertson's clients came by the house that morning. He wanted Mr. Lambertson to make a will for him. On the way there, he'd run into a friend, and the friend had just come from Williamsburg. So Mr. Lambertson got the news almost right away.

"Lord Dunmore kept the keys to the Armory, you know," the client told him. "He didn't want the men from the town to be able to get in. He booby-trapped it too, and he didn't tell anyone. He'd set up guns so that, if anyone entered, they'd be shot.

"Last night, some young men got the idea to break in and take the guns away. Like I said, no one knew the place was booby-trapped with guns. The men were shot. From what I hear, they were hurt pretty badly. Now they say the townspeople are arming themselves. They plan to go back to the Armory and break in, no matter what. Booby traps or no, they want to get the rest of the guns away from Lord Dunmore."

Mr. Lambertson in turn reported what happened to his wife.

"I'm going to town to learn more about it. I want to hear the news more directly. I don't like only knowing things second- or third-hand."

As soon as their father left, their mother turned to them. For different reasons, they were both upset. Amanda blamed Lord Dunmore for setting such a dangerous trap. Amelia blamed the young men of the town for breaking in.

Their mother didn't know what they were thinking. She only knew that her daughters were upset.

"These are difficult times," she told them, "but you two don't have to worry. Whatever happens, your father and I will see that you're all right."

The girls knew their mother was trying her best to reassure them, but she didn't even sound convinced herself.

"Still, you have to be careful," their mother added sternly. "This is no time to take any risks at all. You must promise me that you'll do what your father and I tell you to do, and that you'll always be careful. I couldn't bear it, if anything happened to you."

Their mother looked even more upset than they were. They both ran over to hug her.

"Don't worry, please don't worry!"

"We'll be very careful, we promise!"

After breakfast, they went back to their room to finish dressing.

"You're awfully quiet," Amelia observed, as she helped Amanda into a daytime gown. "What's the matter? It's too bad about those young men, but it's their own fault. They shouldn't go breaking into places they don't belong."

Most days, this would have started an argument. Today, Amanda had a bigger concern.

"I just realized that Father's in the militia," she said anxiously. "If there really is fighting here in Virginia, what happens to him?"

Suddenly Amelia was just as worried as her sister was.

They hadn't thought about it before, but it was clear to them suddenly. If there was fighting, their own father could be in danger. Some men went away to fight and never came home.

A few days later, Mr. Lambertson came home early in the afternoon. He went straight to the library and he looked quite annoyed. He motioned for their mother to follow him there, and Amelia and Amanda followed her.

At first, their father looked like he was going to tell them to leave. Then he had second thoughts.

"You might as well stay," he told them. "You'll hear about it sooner or later. It's not a secret. It's all over town. Lord Dunmore's fled the town. He's left the Governor's Palace to go hide away on one of the warships. The Burgesses tried to tell him it was safe to stay, but he wouldn't listen. He says he fears for his life if he stays in Williamsburg!

"The more he provokes people, the more they prepare to defend themselves," their father continued,

growing more heated as he spoke. "It's a downward spiral. Just a week ago, things looked hopeful. Now everyone is afraid. There are warships just a few miles down the river. It's not just one anymore — there's a whole group of them. Lord Dunmore must have sent for them. There are rumors that hundreds of British soldiers are coming too. Militia are coming to Williamsburg from all over Virginia. They're preparing to fight to defend the town."

chapter 15

Jacob couldn't manage to see Penney as he'd planned. He didn't even give the list to Doctor Galt to look at. He was too busy. In addition to all the usual business, the militiamen were customers now. They wanted to buy medicines. They wanted to buy supplies like bandages, that they'd need if there was fighting. Some had diseases or injuries that needed treatment right away.

When Jacob finally had a quiet moment to talk to Doctor Galt, Amelia's list wasn't the first thing on his mind.

"Will Doctor Mercer come to Williamsburg with the Fredericksburg militia?" Jacob asked eagerly. He'd been apprenticed to Doctor Mercer in Fredericksburg. Doctor Mercer, he knew, was in charge of the militia there.

"I haven't heard whether Doctor Mercer's group is coming or not," Doctor Galt replied, "but it seems like the militia are coming to Williamsburg from pretty much everywhere."

"I want to join the militia too," Jacob said earnestly. "I want to defend Virginia."

Doctor Galt almost smiled at that, but he could see that Jacob was totally serious.

"I admire your desire to defend Virginia, but you're too young. You have to be sixteen. Besides, you're my apprentice and I can't spare you. As far as I'm concerned, that's more important. Any young man can be in the militia. Only some know how to heal people."

"But Doctor Mercer's in the militia — " Jacob protested.

"Yes, I know," Doctor Galt cut in. "Doctor Mercer's a fully skilled doctor, though. You're just an apprentice."

Jacob was crushed. The idea of his joining the militia was never realistic to begin with. Somehow, though, he'd convinced himself it was more than just a dream.

"Now listen to me," Doctor Galt said sternly. "You may think it's very noble and patriotic to defend your country, and it is. There's another side to it, though. When it comes to fighting, it's not romantic at all. It's nasty and terrible. Men get sick, they get shot, and sometimes they die. You only fight if you really have to.

"I'll tell you what," he continued in a milder tone, "if you're so keen to help, we can change your studies. For a few months, I'll teach you about the different kinds of injuries and diseases that military men often get. There are important things that it's good to know. I'll teach you how to do amputations and clean wounds, and how to treat swamp fever. Then, worst comes to worst, you can be helpful. More helpful even than being in the militia."

Jacob cheered up at that.

"Really? Can we start now?"

"We can start as soon as we have time for it." Doctor Galt gestured at the door, where a customer was coming in. "Right now, we have to take care of our customers."

It was only later that day that Jacob remembered the list again. He felt guilty. He realized he'd done noth-ing for Josephine for several days. The next time he had a chance, he promised himself, he'd show it to Doctor Galt.

The chance came at the end of the day. They'd closed the shop and gone to the office in the back. They hadn't stopped working entirely. Doctor Galt was sitting at his desk, keeping up his ledger book, where all the sales were listed, and Jacob was rolling pills. It wasn't hard work, though, so they could talk.

"You know Amanda and Amelia are certain that Josephine couldn't have poisoned Betsey," Jacob began. "I guess they've convinced me. Josephine has been helping people for a very long time and there's never been any problem. So we're trying to figure out what really happened. It must have been something else."

Doctor Galt looked at Jacob over the tops of his glasses.

"Yes?"

Jacob pulled the list from his pocket and handed it over.

"Amelia made this list of things that could cause the symptoms the maid was having. It's a very long list. It includes things that are rare and expensive, and things that are hard to get almost anywhere. They asked me to go over it to see which of these things you could actually get here in Williamsburg. Could you look at it too?"

Doctor Galt took the list and studied it.

"Very good," he commented, when he was done. "It's a very good list for a beginner. I've taught her well."

He looked at the list again and picked up a pencil. He started to cross things off, but then he remembered the ledger.

He put the list aside.

"I'd better finish the ledger first. I'll go over the list when it's not too busy. I can ask some of the others too. I've been thinking about it, and I think it's right to question whether Josephine really poisoned that girl. All we really have is her say-so. Whether Josephine did it or not, we should look into it more. It's the least we can do for Josephine."

chapter 16

"Father, can we ride into town today?" Amelia asked at breakfast. "It's time to see if Mrs. Charlton has my ribbon."

Amanda and Amelia were certain that he'd say yes. They rode into town on their own very often. They were so certain that he'd let them go that they'd even dressed in their riding clothes.

Their father just looked at them, like he was surprised that they'd even ask.

"Don't you remember what I said, that militiamen are coming to Williamsburg from all over?"

They recognized his tone of voice with dismay. They had to persuade him before he actually said "no".

"There were militiamen when we went before," Amanda said quickly. "Everything was fine. We didn't have any problems."

Their father wasn't impressed.

"The situation has changed completely since you were there before. There may have been a few dozen then, but there are hundreds now. Hundreds of men — mostly young men. There's nothing for them to do right now, so they're bored. Bored young men get into trouble. There've been some reports of it already."

Amelia gave her sister a look that said "I told you so."

"I really need to see Mrs. Charlton," she pleaded. She was worried about the militia men, but she wanted her ribbon even more. Maybe this was her last chance to get it. What if things got even worse? "Mrs. Charlton said she'd put the ribbons aside for me. She's expecting me to come and pay for them."

"And Jacob too," Amanda added. "We need to see Jacob. And Penney too. We can't stay home forever! What if the militia stay for a long, long time?"

Their father sighed. It was hard to resist his daughters when they both went after him at once. Plus, what they said was true. Things weren't as dangerous now as they might be, later on.

"All right," he agreed reluctantly. "I'll let you go, if you promise to follow the rules. First, you must stay together."

They both nodded. That wasn't hard at all.

"Second, before you do anything else, you must go straight to see your aunt."

They nodded again. This was anyway what they always did.

"Third, you must tell her exactly where you're going and when you'll come back again."

This was harder. They weren't quite sure how long it would take to do their errands. They thought they could work it out with Aunt Sarah, though. If necessary, they could go back and forth. Their aunt's house wasn't so terribly far from Duke of Gloucester Street.

"Fourth," their father went on, "you must stay on Duke of Gloucester Street. You won't go anywhere else around town unless you have some adult with you. Apart from your aunt and uncle's house, of course."

This rule was even harder. The apothecary and millinery were on Duke of Gloucester Street, but they wouldn't be able to see Penney or Josephine.

They thought about arguing, but they could see from his face that it wouldn't help. They could manage somehow, they supposed. Aunt Sarah was usually very busy, but maybe she'd go with them, if they asked.

"All right," Amelia answered for both of them.

"Fifth, you'll be home by noon."

Amanda looked at her watch. Oh no, that wouldn't work at all! Between riding in and coming back, they'd hardly have any time in town. She opened her mouth to argue, but a better idea occurred to her.

"We need to see Jacob, and Mrs. Charlton too, and Aunt Sarah always likes to see us and talk a bit. Couldn't we stay over with her and Uncle John and come back tomorrow?"

They'd stayed with their aunt and uncle many times. Their aunt and uncle had plenty of room. The house was so big that they each had their very own bedroom. They'd lived there for weeks, when their mother was ill. They'd even left a change of clothes there, in case they ever needed to stay over again.

Their father didn't say anything, so they waited. His silence, they knew, meant he was considering it.

"Oh, all right," he gave in. "Of course you must ask them if you can stay, but I know they're always happy to have you. You still have to be back by noon — noon tomorrow. Tomorrow I'll probably be coming to town myself, so you can come to see me before you ride back again."

The girls gave him a hug and raced upstairs. They'd need some extra things if they were staying overnight.

They each packed up an extra shift, cap, neckerchief, and stockings, plus their combs and extra pins. They took some extra spending money too. With more time, they might do more shopping.

"You see what I mean," Amelia couldn't help but say, as they saddled up their horses. "These men are causing trouble already, just like I said."

"Father's just being cautious," Amanda countered. "Like Jacob said, the militia are here to defend us. They're organized, with officers to keep them in line. It's not like the sailors in Fredericksburg," she added pointedly. Amelia had worked in a shop in Fredericksburg for several years. "I expect the sailors caused trouble all the time."

Amelia didn't have an answer to that. It was true, the sailors caused a lot of trouble. She got on her horse and rode off, leaving Amanda just standing there.

Amanda caught up before long, and soon, it seemed, they were at their aunt and uncle's house. Time passed quickly when they were riding. Because they meant to stay, they took the horses to the field around back of the house, instead of tying them up at the fence in front of it.

Their aunt was pleased to see them, as she always was. She noticed right away that they'd brought extra things.

"Can you stay?" she asked hopefully.

"If we may," Amanda said politely. "It would only be one night. We have to go back tomorrow morning."

Their aunt looked very pleased.

"Of course! It's been quite a while since you stayed over. You can take your things up to your rooms. Then I'll give you some gingerbread, if you'd like it."

Then she changed her mind.

"Or perhaps that could wait. Since you're here, could you first run an errand for me? You could go to the market and get a dozen eggs. Then the cook can make the cheesecake you like so much. It would be good to go now, before they sell them all. Bring them straight back and I'll give you some fresh gingerbread then."

"Is it safe at the market?" Amelia asked shyly. "Father's worried about us coming to town, on account of there being so many militiamen."

"He gave us rules," Amanda added. "We have to stay together, tell you exactly where we're going and for how long, and stay on Duke of Gloucester Street — unless you or Uncle John are with us, that is."

Their aunt smiled.

"Those are good rules. If you follow them, you'll be totally safe. It's good that he's making you be careful, but I wouldn't say things are really dangerous," she added. "You'll be fine running your errands. Most of these men are very well behaved."

That was very satisfactory all around, so Amanda and Amelia took off for the market.

chapter 17

Once they got to Duke of Gloucester Street, Amanda and Amelia could feel the tension in the air. Their father was right. It wasn't like last time. It seemed even more tense than after the gunpowder was stolen from the Armory. When that happened, people were mostly angry, but now there was fear as well. The girls remembered about the warships and British soldiers. They could be coming any day now. Then there'd be fighting. What would happen to them, if they were still in town?

When they got near the market, it got positively scary. There were armed men around the Armory, right next to the market. There were many more of them, like their father said, and they weren't just standing around. Some of them were guarding the Armory, all

of them armed. Others were marching and drilling, like soldiers do. Some of them were standing in lines, practicing how to shoot their guns. At one man's command, they'd load their guns with powder, aim, and then pull the trigger. There was a lot of smoke, and it was very loud and frightening. They didn't seem to be using bullets, but it looked almost the same.

Gathering their courage together, Amanda and Amelia walked right on by them. They sneaked a look at the men, without turning their heads. A couple of the men did look like troublemakers, even to Amanda. Some of them were looking back at them. One of them aimed his finger at them, as if it were a gun, and pretended to shoot them. Then he laughed.

The girls were glad that it was daytime and that there were people all around.

As it happened, going to the market just then was a very lucky thing. As soon as they got there, they saw the very people they wanted to talk to!

Penney was there, shopping for vegetables. She'd already bought some asparagus. They could see the stalks sticking out of her basket.

Jacob was there too, heading towards a butcher's stand.

"Jacob, Penney!" the girls called out to them.

Jacob looked around to see who was calling his name. As soon as he saw them, he came over to join them.

Penney was further away and didn't hear, so the three of them went over and tapped her shoulder. She jumped, but she calmed down when she saw who it was.

"Don't do that!" she scolded them. "You really scared me!"

"We're sorry," Amelia apologized. "We just want to talk to you."

"I want to talk to you too, but first I have to pay for this spinach," she told them, showing them the bunch of spinach that was already in her hand.

None of them really had much time, but they had to stop and talk. It was just too good a chance.

Jacob went first. He pulled the list out of his pocket. He'd been keeping it there so he didn't forget, in case he ever ran into them. Doctor Galt had gone over it and he'd spoken to a number of his friends. By the time he was done, it was a great deal shorter.

"What's that?" Penney didn't know about the list, so Amelia showed it to her.

"These are things that Betsey might have taken, that would have given her the symptoms she had."

Penney looked doubtful.

"Where would she have gotten them? They were pretty careful about that sort of thing at the tavern."

It was a good question, they all knew.

"You said you had something to tell us," Amelia reminded her. "Did you talk to the people at the tavern?"

"Yes, I did, and I'm certain now that Betsey lied about being poisoned. Everyone says that she's the kind of girl who'd do that. If she got into trouble, she'd blame it on someone else. Everyone I talked to said so."

"So why did everyone believe her, when she said it was Josephine?" Amanda was puzzled, like Amelia and Jacob and Penney before.

"Well, there's 'everyone,' and there's 'everyone,'" Penney explained. "The servants I talked to, on the one hand, and the people that mattered, on the other. Betsey's a two-faced girl, one face for some, and another face for the ones who count."

The others understood. No wonder Josephine was so angry. They'd be angry too.

"That doesn't answer the question, though — " Penney went on, "what did she take, that made her so sick? No one I talked to could answer that."

Penney took the list back and studied it.

"I know that the tavern has some of these things in the medicine supplies. I don't know about the others, but it's not like medicines are just lying around there. They keep them locked up in a cupboard. Only Mr. and Mrs. Southall and the head cook have the keys to open it.

"It doesn't have to be something from an apothecary, you know," she added, looking around at the herbs and vegetables for sale at the market. "It could be something in somebody's garden, or even something growing wild. Some natural things can poison you too, if you're not careful."

"Of course! Lots of ordinary things can be poisonous." Amanda was annoyed with herself that she hadn't thought of that. When she was younger, before Amelia came, John the gardener had taught her a lot about the plants in the garden, and also those that grew around them, wild.

"Some things are just plain poisonous," she remembered, "and some things are only safe if you eat the right part, or cook it the right way. Like you can eat the leaves but not the root, or the root but not the berries, or it's only safe if you soak it or cook it."

"There are poisonous look-alikes too," Penney added, "like some mushrooms. Some mushrooms that are good to eat have look-alikes that look almost the same, but they're deadly poison. Even just eating one or two can kill you."

They all looked thoughtful, considering this whole new world of possibilities. Did it make their task easier, or did it make it harder?

Penney broke the silence.

"I've got to get going."

"Me too!" Jacob said, "or I won't have dinner."

"We do too!" Amanda and Amelia joined in. "We have to get eggs too, while they still have them!"

They all hurried off in different directions.

chapter 18

As soon as she saw Amelia come in, Mrs. Charlton opened a drawer and pulled out a little roll of ribbon. She unrolled it to show Amelia.

"Your ribbon came the other day. Here's six yards. That's what you wanted, isn't it?"

"Oh yes! I'm so glad you got it," Amelia said happily. "This one is ever so much prettier than the other. How much do I owe you?" She pulled her little coin purse out of her pocket.

Mrs. Charlton named the sum and Amelia began counting it out. All she had were little coins, half pennies for the most part. She had to count out a lot of them.

While Amelia counted, Mrs. Charlton turned to another customer.

"Things are getting worse here every day," she said unhappily. "We're going back to London soon. I can give you a good discount if you can pay with ready money instead of credit."

"Back to London?" the woman looked at her in surprise. "But what would happen to your shop? You have a very good business here. Would you give all this up?"

"I don't think we have any choice," Mrs. Charlton said bitterly. "Every day there seem to be more of these rebels, these traitors to the King. Remember when there was the Stamp Act, how badly they treated people who were loyal. I'm afraid of what will happen to us if we stay here."

Amelia had finished counting out the price of the ribbon, but she didn't interrupt. This was just what she wanted to hear. Mrs. Charlton thought the same as she did!

The customer looked at Mrs. Charlton with understanding.

"I don't usually say so," she said, "but in confidence, I worry about it also. We wouldn't have Britain to trade with, the King and Parliament to watch over us, and the British soldiers and navies to protect us. How would we ever get by? The colonies don't even like each other!"

"That's just it!" Mrs. Charlton exclaimed, "and all on account of a few hotheads. I admit that there are some problems, but surely they can be worked out.

People haven't even really tried. I can't understand it. All this fuss over a little tea. They've been paying the tax for years without saying anything. Now suddenly it's unbearable. What has changed? And this talk about becoming independent — it's madness! These colonies don't amount to anything on their own. It will be a disaster."

"Lord Dunmore must be concerned as well," the customer observed. "That's why he left town to stay on the warship."

Meanwhile, another customer had come in and heard a bit of the conversation.

"Lord Dunmore is a fool," she said bluntly. "He's perfectly safe here and he knows it. He's causing all this fuss for nothing. He's angry and he wants to get back at the town. I wonder if he isn't causing trouble on purpose.

"And it isn't just about the tea," she added pointedly, looking at Mrs. Charlton. "It's been building up for years, one thing after another. It started out that we were British citizens too, like anyone in Britain. Now we're just local natives to them and they can do what they want to us. We haven't a right to say anything at all. They can just do what they want, no matter what we think or how much it hurts us. You know it's true. They even passed a law to say so."

Amelia was listening with close attention. She wanted to hear Mrs. Charlton argue. Amanda, however, was getting angry. Like the second customer, she wanted to argue back.

"Have you got the money counted now?" she said to her sister, rather loudly.

Startled, Mrs. Charlton broke off her conversation. She'd forgotten they were there.

Amelia gave her sister a dirty look, but she handed the coins over to Mrs. Charlton.

"Thank you, my dear." Not even bothering to count them, Mrs. Charlton put them in a drawer. She gave Amelia the ribbon and turned back to her conversation.

"Why did you do that," Amelia hissed, as they left the shop. "I was listening! I wanted to hear what she was saying."

"You don't need to hear any more talk like that," Amanda scolded her. "How did you get such crazy ideas? How can you not understand what's happening?"

"You call *my* opinions crazy?" Amelia argued back, her temper rising. "Yours are the crazy ones! We're part of Britain. I'm loyal to our King. You're the one who's a traitor."

Soon they were both yelling at each other, insults and arguments, back and forth. By the time they reached their aunt and uncle's house, they'd run out of words and were just silent and furious. Amelia went off to find their aunt, to show her the ribbon she'd gotten. Amanda stormed up to her room.

Amelia found Aunt Sarah in the kitchen. She was seeing how the cooking for dinner was coming along. It looked like a feast was in the making, with all the girls' favorite foods. The cook was basting two whole chickens that were hanging over the fire. In a big pot beside it, she was boiling spaghetti for a spaghetti pudding. There was an iron baking pot with a lid by the side of the fireplace. The girls very much hoped it was there for the cheesecake.

Everything was coming along nicely, it seemed. Aunt Sarah turned to Amelia.

"I heard you and Amanda out there. It sounded like you were arguing. What's going on?"

Amelia burst into tears.

"Oh, Aunt Sarah!" she managed between sniffles, "it's so awful! It's all Amanda's fault and I don't know what to do. She's mad at me because I don't agree with her. She says I don't understand anything — that I'm crazy!"

"What are you arguing about?" Aunt Sarah asked kindly.

"Those people who want the colonies to be independent! I can't understand it and I think they're wrong.

Why are they so upset over a little tea? Britain is our country!"

Aunt Sarah's eyebrows rose. This wasn't at all what she'd expected.

"Amanda doesn't even try to understand," Amelia continued. "She just calls me names. It's not like I'm the only one who thinks this way. Mrs. Charlton agrees with me. She says these people are traitors. She's even going back to London!"

"I see," Aunt Sarah said soothingly. And she did see, more than Amelia realized. But what to say? These were hard questions, in addition to the hurt feelings.

While Aunt Sarah was thinking what she should say, there was a welcome interruption. A ginger cat came in through the kitchen door, with five tiny kittens following closely behind her.

The cook picked up her broom to go after them. The ginger cat was an excellent mouser, but cats didn't belong in the kitchen. Not when she was cooking.

"Get out of here, you beasts!" she shouted, swatting at them with the broom.

Amelia quickly ran over to protect them.

"Please, don't hurt them!"

She gently picked up the mother cat and set her down outside the door. The kittens followed their mother.

"The kittens are so sweet! Can I have one?" Amelia asked hopefully. For a time, her argument with Amanda was forgotten.

Her aunt was relieved. This was much easier to deal with.

"You can if your parents say you can. I'd be happy to find a home for them."

Amelia picked up the very tiniest one.

"This one doesn't look as healthy as the others." She looked at her aunt with concern. "Is something wrong with it?"

"That's the runt," their aunt explained. "It was born last, and it's not as strong as the others."

"Poor thing." Amelia stroked its tiny head with her finger. The kitten curled up in her hand and began to purr very softly. "This one is so sweet. It's the one I want. I'd take good care of it."

"I'm sure you would, and it clearly likes you. You can ask your parents when you get home. In the meantime, I'll save it for you."

Later on that day, Aunt Sarah went to talk to Amanda. She was in her room, reading a book she'd found in their library.

"So you and Amelia have been arguing?" The aunt said it simply, as if it was an everyday thing for sisters to argue. Of course it was, but she knew this wasn't an ordinary sort of argument.

Amanda started to cry, just like Amelia had.

"She called me a traitor! Me, her sister!"

Her aunt frowned.

"I don't think she meant it that way, not so seriously."

"She did! It was something Mrs. Charlton said, and Amelia repeated it. And before, when we were trying to help Josephine, she said I don't know anything. I thought we were so close," Amanda said miserably, "but all this time, I was so mistaken. She really doesn't like me and she's full of crazy ideas."

"Did you say anything to her?"

"Nothing like that!" Amanda protested. "I told her she was wrong. But she is, isn't she?"

Amanda looked to her aunt for confirmation.

"It's not as simple as right and wrong," her aunt said gently. "It's a drastic and risky thing, to talk about breaking away from Britain. For some people, things are fine the way they are, or good enough, anyway. It's not so wrong to worry about what will happen."

Her aunt hoped they'd get over their argument soon, but she wasn't very hopeful. This wasn't an easy argument. People like Mrs. Charlton, calling people traitors, were only making things worse. It never helped things to call people names.

chapter 19

After their meeting at the Market, Jacob looked over the apothecary ledger. He wanted to see what medicines the Southalls had purchased for the tavern. It was a long shot, he knew. Penney had told them that everything was locked up carefully. Even so, Betsey might have found a chance to steal some. The cabinet might have been left open for a while, or a medicine left out to give to someone. She sounded like the kind of girl who might steal something, just because it was valuable. But then why would she actually swallow it?

Penney, meanwhile, decided that she really had to talk to Josephine, even if Josephine got mad at her. Maybe she could get Josephine to tell her what she'd given Betsey.

She knew it wouldn't be an easy conversation.

These days, Josephine spent almost all her time in the kitchen. Given what people were saying about her, she didn't like to go around town. "One of these days I'll overhear someone say something about me," she told herself, "and I'll lose my temper. Then they'll be sorry, but I'll be in trouble too. It's best to avoid temptation."

Josephine was making dinner when Penney came by. It smelled quite wonderful. Luckily, Josephine wasn't too busy right then. The stew needed time to cook and the bread needed time to rise. She was taking a few minutes to sit down and rest herself.

Penney knew better than to start asking questions right away, but she also didn't have much time to spend there. Thanks to Lydia, she had a safe question to start out with.

"Miss Broadnax wants to know, would you share how you make your rice pudding? Do you put in anything special? Someone was over for dinner at the Wythe's the other day and they were saying how good it was. She was thinking to have the cook make it for a dinner party the Wythe's are having soon."

Josephine was more than happy to share.

"I can't say what's special, but I can tell you how I make it," she said cheerfully. "First I cook the rice in milk. Then I add a little nutmeg and cinnamon, and some lemon peel shredded fine. Not too much nutmeg or lemon — they're very strong. You can add as much cinnamon as you like. Then I add some apples, chopped up small, and some egg yolks. You can sweeten it more with some sugar, if you want. Then I tie it up in a cloth and boil it. Usually when I serve it, I add a little butter or a sweet sauce on top."

Penney had a very good memory. As Josephine was talking, she memorized every word.

"It sounds so good," she said when Josephine was done. "I hope the cook makes a lot, so there are leftovers."

Josephine seemed happy at that, so Penney decided to ask her questions. If Josephine was in a good mood to start with, she might not get too angry.

"I heard more about that girl Betsey," Penney began. "The others at the tavern don't think too much of her, I must say. What did she come to you for?"

Josephine's eyes narrowed.

"What are you asking me for?" she said sharply. "Don't tell me you and those fool girls are messing around with this. I told you all not to."

"It's no good, Josephine," Penney said boldly. "You can't tell us not to care about it. We're your friends. We can't just do nothing when you're in trouble. I've heard talk that you shouldn't be giving people tonics and things at all. There's even talk that you should be punished."

For a moment, Penney feared that Josephine would explode. Instead, she just sort of collapsed into a chair by the kitchen table. The way Josephine's face kind of scrunched up, it looked like she might start to cry. That would be even worse, much worse, Penney thought, than her yelling.

Josephine pulled herself together, though. She looked Penney straight in the eye.

"Oh, all right. If you must know, I'll tell you. This girl Betsey was moaning and groaning about all her pains, and how it was making it so hard for her to do things. The way she described her pains, it didn't make sense. I didn't think anything was really wrong with her. So, I gave her some sugar syrup, with a little horseradish added to make it taste and smell bad. I figured that if she didn't like the taste and smell, she'd believe it was really medicine."

"So it wasn't really a tonic at all!" Of all the things Penney had thought of, she'd never thought of this one. "Anyone knows sugar syrup and horseradish couldn't hurt even a baby!"

Josephine nodded.

"That's right. That's why I gave it to her. She was pestering me and pestering me, but I didn't want to give her anything more serious. Like I said, I didn't think that she was really having pains at all. I thought she was making it up to get out of working."

Penney went back to the Wythes, shaking her head in wonderment. Josephine hadn't done anything. Betsey's story was all a lie. That girl deserved to get in a whole lot of trouble. But could they prove the truth?

chapter 20

The next morning, Amanda and Amelia were speaking again, but things were cool between them. Deep down, each was feeling betrayed—how could a sister she loved so much say such awful, hurtful things to her? Talking to their aunt had made them realize how much they'd cared for each other before, but that only made things worse somehow.

Neither of them had time to dwell on it though. They had to get home by noon. They didn't have much more time in Williamsburg.

"It's a pity you can't stay," their aunt said, when she saw them packing up their things. "Your uncle and I love to have you. Didn't you say that your father was probably coming to town today? What if I ask him if you can stay longer?"

Their faces brightened immediately.

Still, it was only a possibility. They weren't one hundred percent certain whether their father was coming to town. He'd only said "probably." And they weren't one hundred percent sure that he'd let them stay (though he probably would, if their aunt was the one to ask him). Just in case, they'd better take advantage of the time that they had left.

They wanted to see Jacob, of course, to find out what he'd learned, and also just to see him. If they could, they also wanted to see Penney. Most of all, they wanted to go exploring. They'd been struck by what Penney said, that not all the poisonous things were in apothecaries. Some of them were in woods and gardens. What could Betsey have found in Williamsburg?

They'd put together a list of the poisonous things they should be looking for, the night before.

Amanda made her own list, remembering the things the gardener had told her. He'd warned her about mushrooms, of course. "Don't you ever go eating strange mushrooms," he'd said, "nor berries either. There's lots of berries that are poisonous. False grapes, yew berries, pokeweed, ivy, and others."

Berries usually ripened in the fall, though. Would any still be on the bushes or vines? She wrote down "berries" with a question mark.

There were plants and flowers too — foxglove and monk's hood and caster bean plant. They were so poisonous that their mother wouldn't even have them in the garden. She was afraid, the gardener said, that Amanda or her sister might try to taste them and get terribly sick or even die.

Meanwhile, Amelia had been looking at a book on plants and herbs that she'd found in their aunt and uncle's library. She'd made a list too, and they put both their lists together. Then they spent some time studying the illustrations in the plant book. They wanted to make sure that they'd recognize the plants if they saw them, so they'd each made a few little sketches and notes.

After breakfast, they set off to see what they could find.

"It's going to be hard to search for things," Amelia complained, "if we follow father's rule that can only go on Duke of Gloucester street. We have to look in fields and in people's gardens."

"I don't think he means we have to stay right on the street." Amanda reasoned. She was good at figuring out ways around things. "That would mean we couldn't even go in the shops, and he obviously didn't mean that. It must mean that we can visit the houses and yards that are along Duke of Gloucester Street."

Amelia approved of her sister's logic.

"So we can look at the gardens, even though they're not right on the street, as well as the ones we pass by on the way from our aunt's house. That gives us enough to look at, I think. Let's get going!"

It wasn't quite the usual thing, to go wandering into people's yards uninvited. They could see a lot from the

sidewalk, however. They also figured — rightly, as it happened — that most people wouldn't mind too much if two young ladies wanted to look at their gardens.

"This castor oil plant is everywhere!" Amelia said after they'd looked in four or five gardens. "Don't people know how poisonous it is?"

Amanda had noticed it too.

"They must like the way it looks," she guessed. "It's so big and has such interesting leaves. John says that the leaves turn purple, and it has big, spiky red balls full of seeds. People like plants that are very showy."

"Maybe that's it," Amelia allowed, "but it seems too risky to me. Those seeds are more poisonous than anything. I can understand better why people grow foxgloves. I like the way the flowers look, with tall spikes of trumpet-shaped flowers. They're in such pretty colors too."

It didn't take too long to find almost everything on their list. There was even some holly and yew that still had its berries.

So their exploring was a success, though it left some questions. Betsey could definitely have gotten some poisonous things, but why would she take them? That was the question they seemed to keep ending up with, no matter what.

Now that their first errand was done, they needed to go see Jacob. First, though, they went back to see their aunt, to find out if she'd found their father and what he'd said.

When they got to their aunt's house, they didn't even have to ask. There was their father in the living room!

They ran over to hug him.

"So you want to stay longer, is that what I hear?" He said it with a smile in his voice and a wink at Aunt Sarah.

From the way he said it, they knew that he'd let them stay.

"Yes, I suppose you can," he said fondly. "In fact, your mother thinks you have a good idea, to do some shopping now when there might be trouble later. If you'd like to, you can even stay three or four days, until your mother and I both come to town. Then we'll all go home together."

With that settled, they all sat down to eat. It was a big meal, with ham, sausages, and chicken pie, along with salad, peas, and mashed potatoes with lots of butter and cream. For dessert there was ice cream — a special treat — and cheesecake with strawberries. They ate slowly, listening to their aunt and uncle and father talk. They didn't have to hurry. Now they had plenty of time.

With so much time, they didn't have to spend every minute worrying about Betsey and Josephine. They decided that they really would do some shopping. Even better, their aunt said that she'd go too.

It was a pleasant afternoon. The weather was perfect, not too hot and not too cool. There was a soft, mild breeze and the sun was shining. They spent some time just walking around Williamsburg, looking at things.

Their aunt didn't have all afternoon free, however.

"I can shop here any time," she told them, "but you're not here that often. Is there anywhere particular that you'd like to go to?"

Amanda spoke up first.

"Could we go to the Printing Office?"

Amelia approved of her sister's suggestion. Dixon and Hunter's Printing Office didn't just print things. They sold books and writing supplies, like paper, quills, sealing wax, inkstands, and pencils. They sold other things too — whatever caught their fancy that they thought people would buy.

Inside, almost everything was on display. Seeing all the ledgers for recording sales and all the Merchant Account books, Amelia was reminded of when she lived with the Browns and helped with their store. What a long time ago that seemed! And then she ended up with Mr. Pryor. All the time that she worked for him, she couldn't remember a single happy day. She prayed that she'd never again go through anything that terrible. She wondered if she'd ever get over it. Deep down, there was a part of her that was still afraid.

Amanda was looking at the playing cards. They'd just gotten a new supply from London. Some were the usual kind, with Kings and Queens and so on, but some had different sorts of pictures.

"Look at this one!" Amanda called out to her aunt and sister. "Every card has a drawing of a different animal! Here's a leopard, and a parrot — and look at the porcupine. Aren't they wonderful!"

Amelia was busy admiring a little pocket notebook. The cover was red leather, with a gold design, and it was just the right size for her pocket.

"That's silly," she replied, not even looking. "How can you play with them?"

"It isn't just animal pictures, of course," Amanda said crossly. "There's a picture of the regular card in the upper corner, so you can tell that it's a King of Spades or a Ten of Clubs, or whatever."

Their aunt admired the cards and the notebook also. Then she bought them for the girls as a present. Afterwards, they went to see a little play that was showing at the theater. It was a comedy, with silly costumes and lots of jokes and clowning-around.

"I'm so glad we saw that," their aunt said afterwards. "I haven't laughed so hard in ages." Amanda and Amelia had laughed as hard as she did, and she was glad about that too.

It was a fine day, despite the shadows of unhappiness. Amelia loved her little pocket notebook and Amanda loved her cards. They both enjoyed the play entirely. Best of all, when they got back to the house, their father had left word that they could each take home one of the kittens!

As much as they enjoyed it, though, so far they'd failed in the main reason for being there. They still hadn't figured out what Betsey had taken. They hadn't been able to help Josephine.

The problem was, they didn't know what more they could do.

chapter 21

"Let's go see Jacob," Amanda suggested the next morning. "Maybe he's learned something. Maybe he has a new idea."

Jacob was there at the apothecary as usual, and Penney was there too. They were standing together at the counter, looking at something. When they entered, Jacob looked up in surprise.

"You're still here? I thought you had to go back home."

"Father says we can stay three or four more days," Amelia answered. "Isn't that wonderful?"

Jacob motioned them over to the counter.

"Come see what Penney's found."

"I didn't really find them," Penney corrected him. "Ned found them."

In the middle of the counter, in a little dish, there were two little beans. They were each about the size of the tip of the little finger, and bright red with a black spot at one end. Amelia reached out to pick one up.

"Be careful!" Jacob cried.

Startled, Amelia withdrew her hand.

"Why? What are they? Is it dangerous even to touch them?"

"Some people call the plant wild licorice," Penney told them. "Some people call it red bead vine or rosary pea. It grows in the islands, in the Caribbean. These are the seeds."

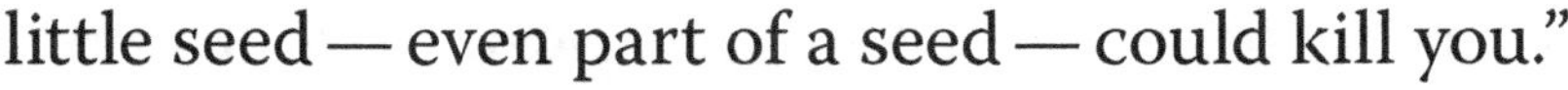

"They're very poisonous," Jacob added. "This hard shell outside won't hurt you, but the inside is pure poison. Just one little seed — even part of a seed — could kill you."

They all stared at the little seeds, amazed. They were so small and pretty, and yet they were so deadly. You wouldn't think so, to look at them.

Amanda broke the spell.

"What are they doing here? Where did Ned find them?"

"That's the really interesting part!" Penney couldn't help but feel excited. "Ned found them on the kitchen floor. I bet it has something to do with Betsey's poisoning."

They all stared at the little red beans again. Was this the answer?

"If they came all the way from the Caribbean," Amelia wondered, "how did they get to Williamsburg? Why were they on the tavern kitchen floor?"

Jacob and Penney both shook their heads.

"I don't know," Penney said. "Maybe we should ask Josephine."

Jacob and Penney were busy, so Amanda and Amelia said they'd go to see her. The Robinsons didn't live on Duke of Gloucester Street, however, and they'd promised. So first they went back to their aunt's house, to see if she'd take them there. Of course, first they had to tell her everything — about Josephine's being accused of poisoning Betsey, and all they'd been doing (and Jacob and Penney too), to find out what really happened.

"So that's what you've been up to." Their aunt looked at them with understanding. "I wondered why you were so keen to stay in town — apart from seeing me and your uncle John, of course. And this morning I noticed that the herbal wasn't in its usual place. Now it all makes sense."

"Please, will you go with us then? It could be really important."

"Yes, I'll go with you," she agreed right away. "I'm curious too."

chapter 22

Josephine knew what the seeds were right away. She also had a pretty good idea how they could get from the Caribbean Islands to Williamsburg.

"They string these seeds for jewelry, necklaces and such," she told them. "Some people just think they're pretty, and some think they're good luck. Some even think they're magic, to keep away the evil eye. Where did you find them?"

"Ned found them in the Raleigh Tavern kitchen, on the floor," Amelia explained. "He gave them to Penney. He knew we all were trying to figure out what happened. He wanted to help you too."

Josephine smiled a little. So many people were trying to help her. It was nice to have so many friends. Then she looked closely at the seeds again.

"See, they've got little holes, one at each end. They used to be strung on something, to make a necklace or some other kind of jewelry."

Aunt Sarah took one of the seeds and studied it too.

"Could something like this have poisoned that girl at the tavern," she asked, "that kitchen maid?"

Josephine got a look in her eyes, like it was all beginning to make sense to her.

"It just might be," she said thoughtfully. "This shell is very hard, and it won't hurt you. When you string it for jewelry, though, the needle goes through the inside. Then the needle can get some of the poison on it. The poison is so very strong that it only takes a little bit to kill you. I've heard stories of people making jewelry who died because they pricked their fingers with the needle. It could be."

"Or sometimes, people chew on their necklaces," Aunt Sarah suggested. "Or you might bite one, just to test it, to see what it like. I suppose if you chewed on one of these and broke the shell, it wouldn't be so good for you?"

"That would do it too," Josephine agreed, "but did Betsey have this kind of necklace? Who would give a necklace like that to her?"

It was a good question, but still they were excited. They felt they were close to finding everything out.

Their aunt suggested that they ought to go talk to Penney right away. So they set off for the Wythe's house, beside the Palace Green.

On the way, they'd all decided that they really didn't need to talk directly to Penney. If she was busy working, they didn't want to get her into trouble. They could just as well talk to Lydia and ask her to give the message to Penney. She needed to ask Ned if Betsey had one of these necklaces. Or maybe Lydia could talk to Ned herself.

chapter 23

It didn't take long for the question to be answered. Miss Cumbo came by the Wythe's the next day. She brought the laundry, and a message too.

"Ned says come by when you can," she told Lydia, "you or Penney. And you can bring that boy with you — the one who works in the apothecary for Doctor Galt."

As soon as she finished her immediate chores, Penney went off to get Jacob. The shop was very busy and Doctor Galt didn't want to let Jacob go at first. As soon as Penney explained what the reason was, however, he closed the shop and came along himself. If this meant that the mystery had been solved, he wanted to hear it first-hand. It didn't seem fair to leave out Amanda and Amelia, so Jacob went off to get them too.

Soon there were five of them, hurrying to the Raleigh Tavern kitchen. They had to wait a few minutes for Ned to be free. They waited outside in the back, all of them very impatient to hear what he had to say.

"You asked about a necklace," he began, once he joined them, "and I remembered something that was maybe related. One of the women who cleans the rooms, Mary her name is, was complaining that she'd lost her necklace. It was about a month or so ago.

"So it made me think," he continued, "and I went back to her. I suggested that maybe she should poke around, looking for her necklace, when she was cleaning up Betsey's room. She thought it was a good suggestion, and guess what she found!"

He paused, pulled a handkerchief out of his pocket, and carefully unwrapped it. In the handkerchief was a necklace. It was made out of rosary peas and little white shells.

"And here it is," he said proudly. "She found it in Betsey's room, all right, though it was hidden. There was a bracelet too. Mary said that the necklace was shorter than hers was, but if you put them together, the necklace and the bracelet, it would be about right."

"Betsey took it apart and restrung it!" Doctor Galt was as excited as any of them. He hadn't known about

rosary peas before, but he'd
done some research after
Jacob showed him the seeds.

"Seems like that's how
it was," Ned said thoughtfully. "Maybe she thought
that would hide the fact that
she stole it."

Doctor Galt took the
necklace and studied it.

"Yes, I think this must be what poisoned her," he
decided. "It all fits. If she stole the necklace, no wonder
she lied and blamed Josephine. She's very lucky that
she didn't die."

"And that's not all!" Ned reached in his pocket
again and pulled out a bottle. "Mary also found this
in Betsey's things. I'm thinking it's Josephine's tonic."

Doctor Galt took it with a smile.

"That's excellent. I think you're right. I recognize
her kind of bottle. I'll analyze what's inside, but I've
no doubt it's what Josephine said — sugar syrup and
horseradish."

"So, I solved your mystery, didn't I!" Ned was beam-
ing. "I guess Miss Josephine owes me one of her famous
peach pies."

chapter 24

They all went back to the apothecary in a triumphant mood. The mystery was solved! Everyone would believe Doctor Galt when he told them what had happened. Josephine didn't have to listen to people saying terrible things about her. She didn't have to worry about being punished for trying to do good.

They wanted to tell Josephine right away. When they got back to the apothecary, though, there were customers waiting at the door. Jacob and Doctor Galt had to take care of them, and Penney had to go back to work.

So that left Amanda and Amelia. They headed off toward the Robinson's kitchen right away. It was blocks away from Duke of Gloucester Street, but they were so excited that they forgot their father's rule. They'd gotten so used to the tense atmosphere and the militiamen that they didn't think about it. Everything seemed quite ordinary and normal.

They quickly learned that it wasn't.

They hadn't gone far before they ran into a group of militiamen. They were standing in a line, blocking the street. There wasn't anyone who looked like an officer, just a group of young men. They were guarding the streets, it seemed, just for practice. They were bored and it was a game, but they were pretending that it was for real.

"Do you have a pass?" one of them asked the sisters.

"A pass? What do you mean a pass?" Amelia looked at them, confused.

"There's no such thing as passes," Amanda added sharply. "If there was, we would have heard."

"Well, there is now," the man told them firmly. "You need a pass, if you want to go this way."

They could see that it was no good arguing, so they turned around.

"And don't try to get around us by going down some other street," he called after them. "We'll be watching to make sure you don't."

They could hear the men laughing at them as they walked away.

"Now you see how right I was," Amelia said smugly. "It's just like I said. These militiamen are just causing trouble. They aren't patriots and they're not defending the town."

"They're prepared to risk their lives to defend us," Amanda shot back. "I call that patriotic. You're just prejudiced. You can't judge everyone by a few young men. They're just bored. It's a nuisance but there's no real harm in it."

Ever since their last big argument, they'd kept on arguing with each other in their minds. They'd been thinking up all their best arguments — why they were clearly right and the other was clearly wrong. Now they said everything they'd been thinking. They didn't hold back. They were so busy arguing and arguing that they forgot to pay attention to where they were going.

Soon they'd lost all sense of direction. They were getting further and further away from Duke of Gloucester Street, and further and further away from Josephine. They weren't even sure where they were exactly. Neither of them had been in this part of Williamsburg for a very long time.

When they stopped for a moment, out of breath from walking and arguing, Amelia happened to glance back.

"I think there's a man following us," she said softly.

Suddenly, the argument took second place.

Wherever they were, there weren't many houses around them. There were mostly fields and gardens. There weren't any people that they could see. There was only the two of them, and the man who was following them. He was coming closer and closer.

They started walking again, faster and then faster still. When they glanced back again, the man was still behind them. He not only matched their speed but, little by little, he was gaining. There was a creepy smile on his face, like he was enjoying their being afraid.

Amanda's heart was beating so loudly that she could hear it. She'd been followed like this once before. Now it was happening again and it seemed the very same. This man was strangely dressed, like the man before had been. His clothes were dirty and didn't fit right, and they were buttoned all wrong. There was a look in his eyes that terrified her. She'd only narrowly escaped, the time before.

Soon the girls were running. As they ran, they looked wildly around. They couldn't see anyone they could go to, and nowhere they could go for safety. There was no one to save them and nowhere to hide.

By pure instinct, Amelia headed for Mr. Pryor's stable — or what used to be Mr. Pryor's stable, before he left town. When she worked for him, the stable had been her only place of safety, and the horses her only joy.

Even though she barely remembered, her feet knew the way. She took a shortcut through one of the yards and it gave them some extra time. For a few moments, the man didn't see them, and they reached the stable door. Amelia frantically opened the sliding door and they slipped inside. Holding their breaths and hoping, they listened as the man passed by.

They waited a little longer, to make sure he didn't come back. Then they took long, deep breaths, and began to calm down.

Looking around the stable, Amelia was flooded with memories. It seemed as if nothing had changed. There was the hayloft, with the rickety ladder to get up to it. There was the bench she used to sit on. There was even a broom in the corner, just like the one she used to use to sweep the floor.

It was like she was working for Mr. Pryor again. It was like she'd gone back in time.

The same old feelings came back to her also, just like she'd felt before. She felt stubborn — though he pun-ished her over and over again, she wouldn't give in to him. She felt angry and afraid. She touched the burn scar on her arm, remembering the pain she'd felt, when she rescued Doctor Galt's

book from the fire. Tears came to her eyes.

Amanda's memories were different but just as strong. When she was chased before by that strange, scary man, she'd found the stable just in time. Inside, there was a servant girl. She had no idea who she was. The girl had told her to hide in the hayloft. So she'd climbed the rickety ladder and hidden behind the bales of straw. When the man came in — looking for a "little thief" he said — the servant girl had stood up to him. As calmly as anything, she'd convinced the man that Amanda wasn't there.

When the man left, the servant girl had laughed at the straw in Amanda's clothes and hair. Then they'd talked. They'd found out they were sisters — sisters who'd been lost to each other for so many years.

If it hadn't been for the scary man and the stable, they might never have found each other. They wouldn't be here together now.

For a long moment, they just looked at each other. Both their faces were wet with tears. They remembered they joy of finding each other, and all the wonderful things that had happened since. They'd found each other, and then they'd found the father that they didn't remember they even had. Now they both had all the family that they'd longed for, for so many years.

They each took a step toward the other, and then another and another. When they were close together, they both reached out. Then they hugged and hugged and hugged each other, as hard as they could. They felt like they'd only just found each other, all over again.

chapter 25

Afterwards, the girls opened the stable door just a crack and looked cautiously outside. They couldn't see anyone around. It seemed that the man had gone. Amanda spoke first.

"We still need to see Josephine and tell her what happened."

"Yes," Amelia agreed. "I know the way from here."

This time, they didn't encounter any militiamen. They got there right away.

Josephine didn't say anything when they told her. There was a special warmth in the way she hugged them, though, and her face just glowed.

Feeling ever so much better about everything, they started back to their aunt and uncle's hand in hand.

"That stable reminded me," Amelia said thoughtfully, "just how bad things used to be. I guess that's why I'm afraid of what might happen if we try to break away from Britain. I don't really think you're a traitor. Mr. Jefferson, Mr. Washington, and the others aren't traitors either, I know that too. I'm just afraid. Like you said before, our father might end up fighting. What if something happens to him? What if we fight and lose?"

"That scares me too," Amanda confessed. Looking back, she felt sorry that she hadn't listened harder. She hadn't even tried to understand. "I shouldn't have said you were crazy. You were right to worry, I see that now. At the time, I was just hurt and angry. I felt like you shut me out."

"I didn't mean to hurt you." Amelia felt sorry too. "I just got wrapped up in making my list. And you weren't being very nice to me, anyway. I guess I felt hurt and angry too."

When they got back to their aunt and uncle's house, everyone was in the parlor — their aunt and uncle, and their father and mother too. The kittens were even there with everyone, snuggled together and purring away on their mother's lap.

Their aunt had told the others how Amanda and Amelia had been arguing. When the girls came in, though, everyone could see that they'd made up again.

The adults continued the conversation they'd been having before the girls came in. They'd been talking about what had happened. It was very big and very serious news. The King had declared the colonies to be in rebellion. The Continental Congress was setting up an army, with George Washington in charge.

What would come next, they all wondered. Would there really be a war?

The girls' father could see that they were listening very hard.

"I know these are very difficult times," he told them, "and I'm proud that you're paying enough attention to have thoughtful opinions, whether people agree with them or not. There are some good reasons to want to stay with Britain, I know, but we can't accept losing all our rights."

Amelia understood better now, but she still wasn't happy about it.

"Could it have come out differently? Did it have to end this way?"

"Possibly," her father answered, "but we'll never know. We tried to find a peaceful solution. The Congress sent a petition to the King, trying one last time. He rejected it. Now we have to follow the path that's laid out for us. There's no choice but to carry on."

Amelia and Amanda thought back over all that had happened, all the good times, the bad times, and the adventures. The future was uncertain, but somehow they'd made it through all their past troubles. They'd make it through again somehow. They had each other, a family that loved them, and such good friends. These were the things that mattered most of all.

The End

acknowledgments

Most of all, I'd like to gratefully acknowledge Emma and Abby Hogan and their brother Sam, who not only have been the models for Amelia, Amanda, and Jacob but who have provided inspiration from the beginning for the series as a whole. I am especially grateful as well to Ann Gates for her invaluable encouragement, wise suggestions, and excellent advice. Thanks also to author and historian Michael Cecere for his thorough research and excellent article on the gunpowder incident (allthingsliberty.com/2020/06/williamsburg-becomes-and-armed-camp-1775).

This series would of course not be possible without Colonial Williamsburg, which provides the perfect setting, the recreation of the real-life characters Lydia Broadnax and Edith Cumbo, and extensive resources for research. The illustrations are derived from photographs, for the most part taken by me but also by other accomplished photographer-reenactor friends. The original photograph of the Portugal Cakes was taken by Frans Verbunt, Shane Kippenhan provided the picture of the Lone Militiaman, and the darling kitchen picture was taken by Karen Fischer House. Most illustrations feature Colonial Williamsburg, but Doctor Galt's desk can be found at the Hugh Mercer Apothecary Shop in Fredericksburg and Amelia and Amanda's house is George Mason's Gunston Hall. Harris Andrews, an expert in 18th writing and publishing, created "the list," Hearth Cook and Food Historian Linda Ziegler created the breakfast scene, and reenactor Sarah Cooper Hrechun posed for Betsey. The horses, Belle and Mallory are modeled after two owned by Kimberly Walters, Jeweler at the Sign of the Gray Horse (https://www.kwaltersatthesignofthegrayhorse.com/) and the pictures of the rosary pea necklace and seeds originated with the United States Department of Agriculture.

Thanks to Stephanie Anderson of Alt 19 Creative for the overall design and formatting, and to my husband Ted Borek, as ever and always, for his patience and loving support.

Since the story is set against the background of actual historical circumstances and events, study questions may be of interest. Look for them at www.Shrewsburypress.com.